I0632762

EARTH, REWIND & FIRE

MISSION 15

BLACK OCEAN: PASSAGE OF TIME

J.S. MORIN

Copyright © 2024 J.S. Morin

All rights reserved. No part of this publication may be reproduced, distributed or transmitted in any form or by any means, including photocopying, recording, or other electronic or mechanical methods, without the prior written permission of the publisher, except in the case of brief quotations embodied in critical reviews and certain other noncommercial uses permitted by copyright law. For permission requests, write to the publisher, addressed "Attention: Permissions Coordinator," at the address below.

Magical Scrivener Press
www.magicalscrivener.com

Publisher's Note: This is a work of fiction. Names, characters, places, and incidents are a product of the author's imagination. Locales and public names are sometimes used for atmospheric purposes. Any resemblance to actual people, living or dead, or to businesses, companies, events, institutions, or locales is completely coincidental.

Ordering Information: Special discounts are available on quantity purchases by corporations, associations, and others. For details, contact the publisher at the address above.

J.S. Morin — First Edition

EARTH, REWIND & FIRE
MISSION 15

THE HOT TUB frothed with soap bubbles, and the ice-cold beer was locally brewed. Carl ducked below the water, holding his breath for a few heartbeats before breaking the surface once again with a gasp.

With a telltale crack that soothed the soul, he popped open his next beer.

After about four beers, give or take a miscounting of scattered cans on the floor, he climbed out of the hot tub and staggered to the balcony. Wet tile floors. A weakened constitution. Bare feet. For an old barfly like Carl Ramsey, this was a piece of cake. Even in July, the night air of Boston Prime chilled his wet skin.

Spread below him, the ancient city and current seat of Earth Empire glittered. Modern and expensive as fuck. Ancient and soaked with bloody history. He had a clear view of Boston Harbor, where for a thousand years and more, humans had boated and fished and dumped sewage. There was even a wooden sailing ship from the ages of antiquity, still floating as a museum.

None of this held his attention.

Eyes to the skies, where billions of stars washed out before the more proximate lights of starships, satellites, and space stations, Carl raised a middle finger that may or may not have been pointed at the Eyndar Empire.

"Fucking missed me again, assholes!" he shouted into the night.

Oh, that felt good. Better than the beer. Better than the shower. Better than the hot tub. Almost as good as the steak. Filet mignon had been a compromise between quality and putting too much food into a stomach that had been too many days without a proper meal. He'd be on porterhouses within the week.

A knock on the door back inside the suite preceded an entrance before waiting for an answer.

"Mr. Ramsey, per your request, the jacket is being restored. The remainder of your attire has been disposed of with, as you also requested, 'prejudice.' I've taken the liberty of acquiring a small wardrobe for your use during your stay."

The concierge was a younger fellow. Proper. A real "checks the work schedule before booking a dinner date" guy. If he were a paying customer at a Squadron 33 1/3 show, Carl would work in some Moody Blues for him.

"Thanks, Roosevelt. What about that other thing?" As he ambled back in—sauntering was still somewhat rough on his hips after sleeping on a slab in an eyndar prison—Carl scanned the floor for unopened beers.

"I have passed along your request."

"Kinda sounds like a 'no.'"

Roosevelt smiled. "If there's anything I can do to make you more comfortable in the meantime..."

"Wouldn't mind just taking a hover for a spin. Nothing

fancy. Just a little joyride, maybe back and forth across the Atlantic."

The smile didn't falter. "I'm afraid that may be too ambitious. However, if you'd like a dessert or something piped in on the holo-projector?"

"I wouldn't mind access to the remote."

"The suite's holo-projector isn't controlled locally, Mr. Ramsey. If you'd prefer interactive entertainment, however, companionship can be provided."

So, no leaving. No access to tech. All the bread and circuses he wanted. "What bush are you beating around? Emperor Khosrau got a guest harem or something?"

"Not in such terms, but I believe you understand the gist."

Carl scooped a beer from the floor before pointing back out toward the balcony. "And if I ran out there screaming that I'm being held prisoner?"

"I'd have already been fielding complaints about your state of undress if the privacy system hadn't adequately sequestered you from outside view."

A bobbing nod and a swig of beer gave him a break to think this over.

"Yeah. All good, Roosevelt, my man. Just checking the walls, if you know what I mean."

"Thank you for your understanding."

He'd swung for the fences and whiffed. Time to slap out a few easy singles. "Here's what I'm really looking for: two slices of cheesecake with raspberry drizzle, a bottle of something at least 80 proof and old enough for a pilot's license, and a masseur with hands like anvils to get these knots out of my back before I try to sleep."

"And for the morning?" Roosevelt inquired. "I could have a steak-and-eggs breakfast delivered, as well as a barber for a fresh shave."

Carl scratched at his shaggy stubble. "Breakfast, yes. Barber, no. I think it's about time I grew the beard back out. Feeling too much like a productive member of society without it. You know?"

Roosevelt's subtle glance up and down Carl's naked, dripping, flabby body, with even his beer gut a deflated balloon from lack of food these past weeks, gave the concierge's opinion.

"Of course, sir. Anything to make your stay more pleasant."

When Roosevelt was gone, Carl dried off and found the last beer from the six-pack he'd requested earlier. If he was going to be kept here whether he liked it or not, he resolved to like it.

━━━

Stars glinted against a backdrop of blackest night. Unseen planets twirled and twisted and rotated and spun about them. All of it took place at ferocious speeds, yet from a distance, it all appeared still and serene. Much like the mind of the wizard who stood gazing at those far-off suns.

Sparta would be back soon, Mort imagined. What would he say to her?

But more importantly, what was he going to say to that little shit Khosrau?

He replayed the conversation in his head.

"*I have Carl Ramsey in my custody,*" that upstart emperor had told him.

Mort hadn't liked the wording of that supposed reassurance. It hinted at extortion. "What could you possibly want for him? I've given you everything in the galaxy."

"*Have you? I'll gladly give you back your only true friend in this galaxy. But I have a price...*"

"I gathered that. Spit it out."

"*Mars. I want Mars back for my empire.*"

"What makes you think I could accomplish that? I didn't when I was in that body."

And that bastard had known. He'd known the secret. "*Yes, but you'd been tied to a chair, more metaphorically than physically, of course. You couldn't gallivant off and just clean house on another planet, no matter how proximate. The eyndar imperial capital may not be as formidable as Earth, but I imagine that Mars won't pose much greater a challenge.*"

"And if I could?"

"*What reason would I have to go back on my word? A bargain is a bargain. Take some time to think it over.*"

And so, here Mort was, doing just as instructed.

That galled him.

The door slid open behind him.

Mort didn't turn. He could feel who it was.

"Ah, you're lost in thought."

"Not lost," Mort assured Sparta as her sandaled footsteps came up behind him. "Wandered farther afield than usual, perhaps, but not lost."

"He's going to turn up, you know."

"Already has."

A jangle of jewelry told Mort that she'd cocked her head in lieu of putting a voice to her mild surprise.

"Got a yell-a-gram from Earth. Khosrau has him. Didn't say how, but I've got ideas."

"You don't look like you consider that good news."

"It's not. He's holding Carl prisoner."

"Did His Majesty offer proof?" She made the formal title sound trite and phony. As if someone had handed him the job and a costume to wear. Which was exactly the case.

Mort harrumphed softly. "Could be lying, but I doubt it. Boy knows better than to try to swindle me."

"But not better than to hold your friend hostage?"

The grumble under Mort's breath would have shaken the ship's hull if he'd raised his voice.

"What do you plan to do?"

It wasn't often that the old wizard was at a loss for words. It was even less often that he was at a loss for actions. "I don't... know yet."

A slender arm snaked around Mort's shoulders and pulled him into a hug. "That's not like you."

"A college dropout with the might of a thousand planets at his disposal has Carl gripped in a fist he could squeeze by accident or design at any moment."

"You should at least tell Jessie."

"I should."

"Are you not going to?"

"At present, no. She'll go off half-cocked—maybe even as little as quarter- or eighth-cocked—if I tell her without including a plan. No, I need advice."

"I've never heard you suggest the idea before. I have to presume you're not referring to me."

"No offense."

Sparta huffed. "None taken. What do I know about prisoners, rescues, and galactic politics? For that matter, what does anyone around here know, really?"

A few steps, and Mort opened a drawer containing pajamas. "You're right, naturally. But you've permitted me my secrets to be doled out over the course of an interesting lifetime or three together, and it's time you learned a new one."

"Ooh," Sparta cooed, clearly trying to express enthusiasm without detracting from the gravity of the moment. "What dark new fact of Mordecai The Brown will I discover this time?"

He shoved a nightgown into her hands, a clear signal that bedtime would be for sleeping tonight. "It's time you met the Council of Ghosts."

━━

Jessie arrived in the Briefing Room at 0905 hours after a sleepless night without the solace of booze or sex to distract her. She couldn't remember the colony name offhand, but there was a mid-core planet with an artsy shopping center, where an ornate glasswork fountain of tubes and spirals pumped colored waters into a basin at the top to filter down and arc out at shopping level for patrons to enjoy. Jessie had been like that all night, but with coffee. She pumped it in constant supply up top and filtered it out again to no observable gain.

She hadn't showered. Hadn't changed. Hadn't so much as spat a mouthful of antiseptic wash to cleanse her breath.

"Call to order," she warned the assembled officers as she made her way to the head of the table.

When Captain Jessica Ramsey was the last one to arrive, it was never a good sign. The table hushed in an instant.

"As of 0855, no credible source has claimed responsibility for the disappearance of retired Earth Navy Lieutenant Commander Bradley Carlin Ramsey," she stated as an opener, as if referring to Dad by his rank and full ID-crystal name could distance him from the lovable dope she'd grown up embarrassed to share a last name with.

Taking the opening, Lt. Cmdr. Schultz stepped in. "Eyndar Empire's all up in arms, but mainly on account of their emperor getting offed in the chaos. Might be it was the heir's faction, might have been radicals, democracy activists, anarchists, or factional infighting. None of them doggos got clue one what's going on round those parts. Prob'ly gonna see a purge soon of them what ain't supportive of the new bloke fast enough. Lotta evidence be going up in plasma soon."

Like accepting a baton, Commander Webber took the handoff. "If we were to throw lifelines to prominent and well-connected dissidents, we might accept answers as payment. However, given that we are—to put it bluntly—*us*, I find it unlikely that we might find willing participants in such a trade."

"I'm willing to entertain the idea of unwilling participants," Jessie stated for the record.

Grosstet gave a brief toot for attention. As if he needed help garnering eyeballs and ears. "IF IT IS STILL POSSIBLE TO INVADE THE EYNDAR HOMEWORLD FOR ANOTHER ATTEMPT, I VOLUNTEER."

"Duly noted." Jessie seethed a sigh. "But until we have better answers, that place is radioactive with political violence. Maybe we can make use of the chaos, but we're in no position until we understand it."

Harmony raised a finger and, at a nod from Jessie, spoke up. "I hate to be the one to bring up the unpleasant possibility. But it is a distinct chance that either the eyndar never had your father in the first place or that he was killed before being swapped for an impostor."

A darkness swept through Jessie's soul. "You think I didn't consider that? You think I stayed up all night because of the peace of mind I had knowing that Carl was out there somewhere having a good laugh at the mess he left his would-be captors in?"

A shake of her head was the only response the doctor offered.

Mindy cleared her throat. "Cap'n? Up to better news, Earth Navy and Mars both ain't any better in the know than us."

"What about the League?" The omission sounded intentional, it was so obvious.

Daphne stepped in. "Since the last time we broke into their comm traffic, Phabian has upgraded their security protocols. It'll be a few hours before the *Arete* computers break the new encryption. But Phabian gains nothing from interfering, so while we'll follow up, there's no reason to expect they'll be involved."

Jessie hated that answer, but she couldn't help agreeing. Phabian had been the only sympathetic major government since Jessie had gone on the run, and they cooperated in ongoing efforts to resettle the refugees from Ghenlar Par'Mol on New Garrelon.

Instead of focusing on what they could prove, Jessie shifted the subject. "Motives. Who gains from Carl's disappearance from that execution festival?"

"Us?" Trebla suggested. "I mean, Uncle Carl had no way to know we were planning a rescue. If we hadn't snatched some eyndar corpse off that miserable rock of a planet, we'd be thanking various gods and bookies that someone else did it for us."

The door opened, but Jessie was already set on replying. "There's not evidence one way or the other that Carl was ever even *on* the eyndar homeworld. All we have are—"

Hadrian, who'd been the one to enter through that open door, interrupted. "He was. He isn't. And I can explain how and why."

Jessie resisted the urge to roll her eyes. Lurking just inside the doorway as the wizard entered was his consort, girlfriend, or keeper, depending on what passed between the two of them behind closed doors. If he'd had a revelation, Jessie could only guess that it was either some crazy Uncle Enzio–grade theory or the magical machinations of that worthless seer of his.

Folding her arms, Jessie promised herself she'd listen to anything at this point, no matter how far-fetched.

———

Mort waited until he had the attention of every set of eyes in the room. He confirmed every pair but Sparta's, confident that not only was she paying attention, but she already knew what he was planning to say. She might not have been able to *see* his future, but she could damn well hear it just fine when he told her on the way here.

"Carl is alive."

"This better not be one of those 'if he were dead, I'd know it' shticks." Jessie was forgetting herself. Or at the very least, she was forgetting him.

"No. I have an announcement to make." Mort paused for dramatic effect. "I have been contacted by Emperor Khosrau. He has Carl. He's willing to barter for his safe release."

Cries from all around the table expressed confusion, disbelief, relief, and yet more confusion.

"How's it the emperor's got a comm ID for you?"

"Why would Emperor Khosrau care about Carl Ramsey one way or another?"

"THIS IS EXCELLENT NEWS, CORRECT? A GREAT RELIEF TO KNOW YOUR FATHER IS SAFE."

"Color me skeptical. Sounds like someone around here pulled a cruel prank."

"In what galaxy's the bloody emperor ringing up a wizard with the ink on his sheepskin still wet to do business?"

"Hey, don't look a gift father in the mouth, am I right?"

Jessie maintained a blade's-edge focus on him the whole while. "Just what is he looking to barter? I can't hand over the ship."

"Luckily, that prospect never came up," Mort replied.

"Good. Well... what *does* the bastard want?"

"Mars."

"WHAT?!" Though Jessie was among the protesting throng, she was far from the only one shocked at the price.

"Uncle Carl's a good guy, but I think we can probably haggle the emperor down to a border colony," Trebla suggested.

"Bollocks, he might as well tell us to sod off as ask us to conquer a bloody planet. Shittin' in the eyndar's boots is one thing. If we could go knockin' round a planet the size of Mars, don't they think we'd have bloodied their noses by now, leastwise?"

Mindy had a fair point, but she wasn't fully informed.

Neither was Harmony. "I have a hard time believing Emperor Khosrau is delusional enough to think Hadrian was in any position to deal for Mars."

"Oh. I am," Mort assured them. Even as the conversation had shifted to half a dozen side discussions of the prospect of getting Carl back by freewheeling trade, deception, force, or stealth, the wizard made himself the center of attention once again.

"Seriously?" Jessie asked, eyes open as wide as they went. She was asking a different question than the one the others heard, and Mort gave a tiny nod in reply.

"I have a confession to make. Cat's been scratching up the insides of this bag far too long. Time to let the poor thing out. I am Mordecai The Brown."

"Who?" Mindy asked before the stunned silence had time to linger.

"That's not funny," Harmony informed him.

Trebla forced a chuckle. "Yeah. Um. From a certain point of view, maybe it is?"

"Though I've done a lot of soul-searching as a result, bear in mind that I manhandled Hadrian even before upgrading my physiology," Harmony pointed out.

"I wasn't using this form at the time," Mort replied evenly. "That was Hadrian, my grandson."

"What... uh... happened to Hadrian?" Daphne inquired, meek as a mouse.

Mort's scowl had several attendees leaning back in their seats to be just a teensy bit farther from him. "He's holding Carl captive on Earth."

"Wait, what?" "How?" "Does that mean—?" "But then—?" "I don't understand what's going on here!"

Mort let the questions fly, circle around a while, and land before explaining. But just before he launched a soul-cleansing admission, Mindy once more beat him to the punch.

"Just who even *is* Mordecai The Brown? Haddy's grandad, right? But other than that, should I have heard of the bloke?"

"He was notorious a long time ago," Harmony declared.

"The notoriousest."

Charlotte jumped in with, "And an old family friend of the Ramseys, I've come to understand."

"The oldest."

"One of my father's old cronies," Jessie chimed in.

"The croniest."

Daphne pointed past him to Sparta. "Did *she* know?" The question sounded more like an accusation.

And Mort wasn't the one who answered. "He told me before we moved in together at school. I consider myself the primary beneficiary of his youthful physique. Anyone who's ever dated a boy of academic age can relate to the feeling that all that vigor, libido, and visual appeal are wasted as a mask for insecurity, ignorance, and pleas for external validation. Instead, I get history's most dangerous wizard looking like *this*."

Mort suffered the presentation of himself as some kind of

object of desire. Frankly, Sparta appeared to be the only one holding that opinion of Hadrian's appearance, and that included the fellow in the mirror staring back. Sure, he wasn't a wrinkly, liver-spotted human leather sack of bones, but she clearly saw him as something he wasn't.

"History's?" Mindy echoed incredulously. "If'n he's such a big deal, you'd'a thunk we'd'a heard of him in non-magic circles, eh?"

"Oh..." Charlotte spoke with a thespian's knack for the melodramatic. "The Convocation can be *quite* keen on sweeping embarrassments under the flying rugs. But what I'd like to know is... how long has Eric known?" She left a lingering note of menace, as if, in some alternate version of reality, she posed any kind of threat to him, even obliquely.

"You've picked up your mother's flair for the villainous. I'll grant you that much. And maybe, just maybe, you could have bullied Hadrian into spilling his guts. But if you want to know when Eric's mind sorted out a puzzle for which he possessed far more pieces than you, you'll have to ask him yourself. Just know that while he hates keeping secrets, he's damnably good at it, and it wasn't his secret to reveal."

"So, what?" Jessie demanded, yanking the conversation back to the practical. "You admit you're Mordecai The Brown, formerly the galaxy's most wanted magical criminal. Great. How does that get Carl back?"

"I'm still not even sure I believe him," Harmony admitted. "It's a con man's trick. For all we know, Hadrian got himself stronger by convincing other wizards to think he was Mordecai The Brown, and now he's trying to leech gravitas off the rest of us."

Mort was prepared for the skepticism. "I taught your mother magic. Well, the rest after the pittance she'd picked up from her school friends. I know her better than you do."

Harmony scoffed, but Mort continued. He aimed a finger at Trebla. "Your father figured me out when I was Enzio Stiles. Best technologist friend a wizard could ever ask for, and if you tell him that, I'll deny every word." He pointed that same finger Jessie's way, more for the benefit of the others than her directly. "As for you, I've known your father since before he was legally allowed to do a great many things he did anyway. I know secrets about him that I'll take to the grave and vice versa. But if any of you needs *proof* that I'm Mordecai The Brown, the carnage in the eyndar capital ought to be proof enough."

"I mean, who's to say what's magic and what's them eyndar at each other's throats?" Lisa suggested. "Hovers and patrol ships shootin' each other down. Explosives detonating. Place was a fucking war zone."

"I was angry."

"You was angry?" the ship's acting security chief echoed.

Mort shrugged. "At the time, we were waiting for Jess to summon the shuttle to get us back with the body of my best friend, desperate enough to let Victoria Frankenstein over there take a crack at reanimating him. I crashed those airborne contraptions. I melted the prison. I turned their imperial palace into a barbecue smoker. Me."

"Lot of them was prolly innocent people," Mindy protested. "Just doin' jobs. Followin' orders. Mindin' their own."

"On whose authority do soldiers kill?" Mort countered.

"Officers. Chain of command and all that."

"On whose authority are convicts executed?"

"Judges. Courts. Them shites as got appointed the job."

"And what gives them the right?"

"I... uh... they's got a mandate. A mandate. That's it. Orders from the top. Laws. All that rot."

"I've been at the top. It's all excuses up and down. If

someone wants to kill, they kill. If someone's too afraid of the fallout, then they don't want it that badly. All orders and laws do is give a clear path to people already willing or eager to kill who might otherwise worry about getting punished for it. I don't worry about punishment. The Convocation's wanted me dead since before anyone around here but Uom'pe and Grosstet were born. And they stopped trying before they thought someone had done the job for them, simply because *they* worried about the consequences of any more trying."

Trebla looked to the senior officers while hooking a lower thumb at the wizard. "If he's not Mordecai The Brown, I'm willing to let Hadrian get himself killed trying to pretend."

"Fine. Say we believe you," Harmony granted him. "What does that even mean?"

"It means he believes that I could destabilize the Martian Military Government."

"How?" Lisa asked. "If'n it was so easy, why not do it before now?"

"By killing most, if not all, of the top officials. I've been busy. First, I was running an empire with vipers in every closet and knives behind every back. When I got a hapless dupe to take the job, I finished up his senior year of college so I'd at least be able to call myself a wizard.

"It's been a busy year."

―――

"Eric, I think we need a chat."

The young chronomancer stared at the ceiling, fingers laced at the back of his neck as he lay atop the otherwise neatly made bed. He could tell by Charlotte's tone of voice that something was wrong, and given the events of the last few thousand copies of yesterday, he could well imagine some of the options.

Rather than commit himself down the wrong conversational waterslide, he gave a noncommittal answer. "I'm available for chatting."

"Don't start with me," Charlotte warned, her heeled boots clacking on the floor on her way over to him. The mattress bounced and sagged him toward her as she perched beside him and looked down into his eyes. "How long have you known he was Mordecai The Brown?"

"That one's a little complicated."

"I'm perfectly capable of assimilating complexities. Enlighten me."

Eric blew a long sigh. "I can't say *exactly* when I first put it together. When I was a kid, just learning magic, I realized that Enzio Stiles was a phony ID. But that was just a suspicion. When I got up the courage to ask, he admitted it. I kept that secret for... I don't know, ever since. Trying to measure time just feels increasingly pointless and arbitrary. It was a secret. I kept it."

"Even from your parents? Even from Jessie?"

Supine shrugs didn't seem to carry the same degree of equanimity as standing shrugs, but he offered one nonetheless. "Mom didn't need that weird thought in her head. I never talked to them about it, but once I knew, I could kind of pick up vibes that Dad and Uncle Roddy both knew, too."

"Well, now the whole crew knows. Or, at any rate, they all will once Makket blabs it to everyone in Logistics. But what about the intermediate step? You knew he wasn't Hadrian when he came back."

"Hard to pinpoint, but there's just a Mordecainess. It's like watching an animated holo and recognizing one of the voices from something else. You go in letting the holo fool you, letting it convince you the cartoon bears can really talk. Then, all of a sudden, one of them laughs and a little candle lights in your brain. You know that laugh. In that instant, you realize... Bertram Birdie from Birdie's Treehouse. Now, you're looking at a bear and hearing a bird and the spell is broken. That's how it is with Mort. I've known him for centuries. My memories from Mortania—his littler version of the Village of Eternity—stick better in my head."

Charlotte brushed a few stray strands of hair from Eric's face. "And him being Emperor Khosrau Blackstone?"

"I never met the emperor in person. It was just a guess."

"No one would guess that. No one would *think* to guess that."

"I blurted it to Jessie when it first came to me. Not Mort, mind you, since she didn't know about that part, but Uncle Enzio. She didn't believe me, which was lucky. I guess? In any event, it feels good not having to pretend I don't know anymore. Sorry I couldn't tell you."

"A secret such as that one... I don't know that I could have trusted you with my own if I knew you could divulge something so private and dangerous for mere love."

Mere?

The hurt must have shown in his eyes, because the next thing Eric knew, Charlotte had bent down and rested her forehead against his, eyes closed.

"Eric, love is precious and priceless, but it isn't a balm for all the galaxy's ills. Love doesn't conquer all. It isn't all one needs, despite that insipid song. So much tragedy and so much stupidity are the result of love run amok. It is possible to love so deeply you lose all reason and sense of self, and that is something twisted and ugly, not beautiful. A sentient creature needs convictions, ideals, integrity. To be all outward spewing love is to become unlovable. I don't want a faucet spewing adulation my way. I like having a curious little treasure chest that lets me peek inside when I ask nicely."

"So... you're not mad?"

"I've attempted being angry with you over this whole affair, but I can't find fault in your actions. I've been left in the dark because the light you were given was for your eyes alone."

"I take it that this isn't a 'no more secrets' talk?"

"We're not caricatures in some romantic holovid. You've seen the dusty, disreputable corners of my psyche, but I still have nooks and cubbies you may never delve. I daresay you have whole worlds swirling in that imagination of yours to which I'm not privy. Let's keep some mystery and trust one another's judgment over what to share."

Taking him by the hand, Charlotte hoisted Eric into a seated position for a good long hug.

As he clung to her, Eric decided that the time loop wasn't a topic he needed to share.

Harmony's morning had been a parade of frustrations. Mindy had shown up for a checkup deficient in molybdenum due to a three-day deviation from her assigned diet. She'd had to replace half the blood in one of the Logistics workers after a workplace accident resulting from a violation of the safe stowage protocols Chinochin had implemented. Newsfeeds had reported that one of her executive assistants had been executed for collaboration with Harmony Bay offices on Earth. And to top it off, her neurochemical balancing subroutine had kicked up an error for excess cortisol buildup.

It had all started with that damned meeting.

Mordecai The Brown...

While, deep down, Harmony knew that but for a wild confluence of implausible events, her own life would have turned out vastly different from its present course, she couldn't overlook the demolition laser that wizard had taken to her family.

Namely Mom.

Esper Richelieu could have slunk back to the One Church, done a freighter-load of penance, and been forgiven her trespasses. She could have taken her rescue from the *Mobius* and Jessie's family and hopped off after realizing she wasn't cut out for a life of crime. She had a college degree and a pretty face, and much as it hurt to admit, that combination could buy a lot of second chances.

But Mordecai The Brown had turned her into a wizard.

Harmony's knuckles whitened as she gripped her datapad just considering that such a malevolent, manipulative, *dangerous* bastard was aboard the *Arete*, where Grosstet had done such an admirable job instilling a sense of herd to this rabble.

From behind her, large, strong hands slipped the datagoggles off her face.

Harmony spun her chair around. "What do you think you're doing?"

Britney aimed a spare finger at the monitors, where Harmony's own vital signs were on display. "Intervention, Doctor. Exam Room 2, stat."

"Excuse me? I have work. As you can no doubt see for yourself, my neurochemical imbalance is in no state for foolishness."

"Yup. And you can program an H-tech fix for it later. Right now, we're going to fix those readings manually."

"Manually?" Harmony echoed as she reluctantly went along with being towed from her chair and down the short stretch of hallway separating her office from the examination room in question.

When the pair arrived, Harmony instantly saw the configuration of the table and knew what was in store for her. "I don't have time for a massage."

"You had two more appointments before lunch. Neither urgent. I rescheduled them for you."

"Where do you get off—?"

"You look after the crew. I look after you. That was the deal. I don't care if you can spend the morning tinkering with your brain chemistry from your datapad. Right now, you're irritable and I'm putting in a fix."

Before sniping back and proving her assistant's point, Harmony examined her recent words and actions. The actions didn't have a chat log, but she could bring up a listing from her datagoggles of everything that had been said in the past few minutes.

It wasn't a good look.

"Fine," she relented. With the door closed and only Britney with her, Harmony pulled off her top and lay face down on the table, placing her chin, cheeks, and forehead against the padding of the support cutout and pawing around underneath for the armrests.

She heard the wheezy squoosh of a plastic bottle and a pair of hands rubbing together. Then, those hands dug into the flesh of her exposed back, and Harmony felt the inert tension in every muscle from splenius capitis to external oblique stubbornly resisting.

There was no massage oil in Med Bay's inventory. Whatever Britney was using had notes of apricot and coconut and warmed her muscles more than the lubrication-reduced friction alone could have produced.

Attempts to organize her afternoon in her head faded amid waves of relief as the coiled, overwrought muscles relaxed.

"Lemme know if I'm going too hard on you," Britney warned. "We're both of us made of more than regular muscle these days."

"'Sfine," Harmony mumbled.

"Well, you feel anything you don't like, just say the word."

"Kay."

How could Harmony object? She couldn't remember feeling this good. Emotionally, sure. Xrista's first day of life flooded her with a joy she could only *hope* to match with the emergence from incubation of a second daughter. But physically?

"Hips up, unless you're ready to be done?" Britney suggested with a mix of order and inquiry.

Groggy and relaxed, Harmony played along. An unclasping. A quick zip. Her pants slid down past feet that had, at some point she'd failed to notice, lost their shoes.

Thighs. Calves. Every square centimeter of her feet. Those roving, firm, impossibly warm and soothing hands ventured everywhere, leaving bliss in their wake.

How long the attention lasted, Harmony could only guess until she retrieved her tech. But it was over all too soon.

Deft hands tugged, and she felt the cinching of her bra strap, followed by a playful slap on the lower back.

"Up and at 'em, Doctor. All done."

Blinking as her circulatory system resumed normal function, Harmony pushed herself up to a seated position and accepted her neatly folded uniform. "You sure we couldn't go a while longer?"

"Back's all done. Front and insides are extra," Britney joked with a wink as she washed up. "You're sounding a lot better, at least."

"That's the best thing I've ever felt in my life."

The water in the examination room sink stopped. "Ever? Like, *ever* ever? You're grading on a curve or trying to fluff my ego, right?"

Harmony shook her head. "Nope."

Her assistant passed her hands under the evaporative dryer. "You know there's other things that are supposed to... you know... be a lot better than that, right?"

By this point, Harmony had given up on an extension of the massage and begun dressing again. She rolled her eyes as she stepped into her pants. "Of course. And I've experienced a variety sampling. Gave up on it long before Xrista came along."

Britney cleared her throat. "Not to step out of line, but... are you certain you were doing it right?"

Harmony huffed as she slipped her shoes on. "I will allow that I did not conduct any kind of scientific inquiry into the matter. Monitoring my own neurochemical levels pre-, post-, and mid-coitus might have suggested advantageous improvements in methodology, but the equipment wasn't freely available to do so during medical school, and I doubt permission would have been forthcoming. Plus, I already had a dresser drawer full of—you know what? I don't know why I'm telling you all this. I'm probably loopy from an influx of endorphins, and *now* I most certainly can look up a real-time view of my brain chemistry if I can just—"

But Britney snatched up Harmony's datapad, holding it aloft and out of reach. Her datagoggles were on the counter on the far side of her much larger assistant. "You need to stop managing your brain like it's a machine and just let yourself feel."

From tiptoe, Harmony couldn't reach past Britney's elbow to get at the datapad, but that didn't stop her from trying. She hooked an arm around a shoulder for leverage. Another arm, not her own, wrapped around to halt her climb. "If you'd just let me—"

Eyes met.

Eyes closed.

Lips met.

Harmony felt as if she were floating, but her feet really *were* off the ground. She pointed her toes upward, daring Britney to let go and drop her a full meter right onto her knees. But Britney clung to her.

When Harmony gasped for breath, the two pairs of eyes met again. Britney leaned, a prelude to setting her boss gently back on the floor.

Impulse struck. Harmony threw her legs around Britney's hips and hung on. The slight boost in height lifted her just taller than her assistant. She laced her fingers at the back of Britney's neck and kissed her once again.

Time passed weirdly, measured in brief intervals of heavy breathing. But something had been unleashed inside her, and Harmony didn't know that she dared try to cram it back in its cage in this state.

"How long until that rescheduled appointment?"

Britney's shrug jostled her. "Couple hours. Ish. I could check a chrono if you—"

"You have until then to do whatever you want with me. Anything. Don't even ask. Just do. And that includes sending a comm straight to the captain reporting me for a mental breakdown or harassment. I just... I can't... I mean... I've never..."

"You sure?" Britney asked calmly, eyes locked with her boss's.

"You know what you're doing, I assume?"

Britney nodded.

"Then do it. Whatever it is, just do it."

Stumbling around the examination room, the pair bumped into the table, where Harmony found herself deposited. Barely taking breaks for air, they resumed the process of clothing removal, this time for both of them.

Uom'pe and Aubrey had delivered all the plates and platters, the serving bowls and pitchers of Grosstet's beer. Everything for a formally informal dinner in the captain's quarters looked so out of place in Jessie's spacious squalor. In all her time aboard, she'd never prioritized taking seriously her job as the figurehead of the crew. All business. A little pleasure. No pomp beyond what her uniform lent her.

But once the guests arrived, the implication that this would be a stilted, formal meal vanished.

Eric arrived with Charlotte, both wearing matching fuzzy pink slippers for reasons that Jessie promised herself not to investigate. A hug from each, and they took their seats.

Not long thereafter, Hadrian and Sparta showed up. Jessie's brain still hadn't fully acclimated to the fact that she'd known this person longer than Eric had been alive. He'd told her bedtime stories, covered her ears when Squadron 33 1/3 concerts grew too loud for her, and ensured that the Tooth Fairy paid out on time. The fact that cranky old Uncle Enzio, Dad's drunk wizard buddy and family tagalong, had been both Mordecai The Brown and Emperor Khosrau and now joined her dinner table in Hadrian's trade-up body was a jigsaw puzzle where all the pieces were round. Nothing fit, and nothing looked liable to fit anytime soon.

"Thank you for having us," Sparta told her. This one was the mystery. If Hadrian was a puzzle, she was an enigma. She purported to *know* all these secrets about Hadrian—or should

Jessie really start referring to him as Mort?—and yet acted like it was perfectly natural. A nasty little corner of Jessie's brain speculated that she had enough trouble finding men taller than her that she wasn't about to be picky about murder and body-snatching.

Eric burst forth with words before Jessie could think of a gracious response. "It's nice to be able to have a big family dinner. Dad never really liked performative eating, as he called it—*calls* it. And Jessie doesn't like eating with just me because I slurp soup and hold my fork the wrong way and—"

A raised hand cut off the growing tirade. "Yeah, yeah. I get it. I complain."

"You'd think chow hall with the marines would have inoculated you against crudities of all manner," Hadrian pointed out as they all surrounded a table set with food that all of them had yet to touch.

"They weren't marines," Jessie reminded him through gritted teeth. If he was doing this just to prove he'd been Enzio Stiles, it was working. "I was in Earth Navy Special Forces."

"Potato, potahto," Hadrian countered.

Charlotte snorted. "A combined thirteen years of Oxford education, and the lot of you choose wrongly."

The door slid open once again. Trebla hustled in, followed by a reluctant Jasmine. They both wore fresh uniforms and Jasmine's hair glistened with the dampness of a recent shower and skipping the omni-dry.

"Sorry we're late," Trebla announced.

"Wouldn't be a family dinner without you," Eric called out with a big grin.

The pair took the last two places around a table set for seven. The three couples only reminded Jessie that she'd chased away anyone who'd have made for an even eight.

"Dig in, everyone," she told them. While the *Arete* was a

heavily herbivorous vessel, Uom'pe's kitchen served some really nicely prepared roast beef when it was available. Jessie had always relished the job of carving meat and had a good deal of experience with blades of all sorts. She passed out thin slices of rare beef as the others heaped piles of mashed potatoes, grilled asparagus, and fresh-from-the-oven dinner rolls on their plates.

Small talk broke out amid the passing of side dishes and apologies for reaching arms. Half her guests, Jessie knew all too well. Their partners were less familiar, initiates into the oddity of Ramsey family relations. None of the couples was married. The only legal or biological bond tying any of them together was between Eric and Jessie, brother and sister. The others were indistinctly related, adjunct family that was no less real.

Was Trebla a cousin? Not by any genealogist's or biologist's definition.

Was Hadrian an uncle? Not by three hermit crab moves between bodies and a lack of even a marriage to tie him to the family before that.

But Jessie wouldn't have hesitated when asked if they were family. Of course, they were. Even if Hadrian's whole deal was more than she could wrap her mind around.

Before everyone had arrived, Jessie hadn't known how she'd try to steer the conversation. But if she'd worried at all that the meal would turn awkwardly silent, she'd have worried for nothing.

Wizards only kept their mouths shut when they wanted to appear mysterious and enigmatic. Trebla couldn't help sniping with little comments that each attempted to prove his wit and humor.

And Hadrian reminded everyone repeatedly that he was Mordecai The Brown and had known Carl Ramsey since he was a boy.

"And then, get this. We find him in the rec room, scooping

up loose terras that the other pirates had been playing poker over. I swear, if we hadn't shown up to rescue Carl and his pal Drew, the two of them would have been *running* that pirate outfit before they were old enough to drink legally on a core world."

"How many of your stories about Dad involve pirates?" Jessie asked.

Charlotte paused just before taking a sip of beer. "Fewer than my mother's, I daresay."

"Oh, I wouldn't put a number on them," Mort countered. "Boy or grown man, Carl attracted pirates like a lodestone. Why, when I heard you were using this bucket to hunt pirates, my first thought was that if you tied your father to a fishhook and dangled him in the Black Ocean, you'd catch your fill of the bastards lickety-split."

"Uncle Carl being a starfighter pilot was already a stretch for me," Trebla commented, mouth full. "Him being a pirate and a syndicate lieutenant and a war hero just won't stay between my ears." He washed down a swallow from a pitcher of water that had become his to share with his date; they were the only ones not drinking beer.

Jessie took note of Jasmine's silence throughout the meal. As captain, certain aspects of therapy weren't sealed to her. Charlotte had to keep her apprised of at least a basic level of mental well-being. The fewer people the young engineer was around, the easier it was on her. Jessie had hoped that seven would have been few enough, but a boisterous, confident, and historically murderous guest list had stuffed her back into her shell.

But Charlotte was the one who tried to bring her into the conversation. "We've all of us had our preconceptions of the elder Ramsey. As someone who hadn't been forewarned of his nature, what was your impression when you met him?"

Jasmine froze. Only her eyes and jaw moved as she chewed and swallowed before answering. "Honest opinion?"

"Oh, do tell," Sparta coaxed. "Anything that requires precaution is worth revealing in close company."

Jessie gave a nod. Eric looked expectantly. Mort feigned indifference as he gorged his young body on delicious fare.

"I kind of got the impression he was hitting on me. Except I couldn't say for certain."

"Oh, that sums up Dad," Jessie assured her. "I didn't pick up on it until puberty, but I swear the guy patted himself on the back every day for how many women he *didn't* cheat on Mom with."

Mort grunted with his mouth full.

Jessie didn't follow up. Odds were, if any of her own preconceptions, inferences, or deductions about her father were off base, she imagined the wizard knew certainties.

They stuffed their faces and swapped stories and scratched at the layers of veneer the newcomers still sported. Stick around the Ramseys long enough, and the facade would all be chipped away in time. But it would take more than a single meal.

A sly comm to Logistics got them a cheesecake delivered. Another got freshly brewed Ganymede coffee for afterward.

And it was only as the coffee was wrapping up that someone finally cracked open the lid on the topic that might end the meal abruptly.

"So, Mort..." Trebla tried out the name, still feeling his way around it. "Are you really considering overthrowing the Martian Military Government to get Uncle Carl back? Not gonna lie; it almost felt like all those stories... we were mourning him a little."

"Mourning?" Mort balked. "Ha! That scofflaw has a hall pass from the Grim Reaper with Rasputin's name scribbled out and his own penned in place of it. But no, I don't see that a Martian coup would convince that rotten grandson of mine to return Carl."

A hand that had been clenched around Jessie's heart released. Until that moment of melancholy relief, she hadn't even felt its presence. This was permission to stop believing. To stop hoping for miracles and accept her father's fate.

Mort dabbed the corners of his mouth with a starched white napkin that had spent the meal in his lap. "No. I don't think that would work out at all. We're just going to have to topple the damned empire and take him back by force."

━━

Morning came, and Sparta had made herself scarce at Mort's request. He'd shaved and showered and dressed but not eaten. Sex for breakfast was her idea originally, and while skeptical at first, Mort had come around on it. While it didn't quell the nagging of an empty belly, it certainly sated *one* hunger, at least.

Moderately hungry but not debasing himself by complaining, Mort waited as Trebla fiddled with the comm panel in the wall, hands tucked into his sleeves.

"Gimme just a sec..."

Mort had no intention of interfering.

"OK, so I just—"

An explanation ensued, but the verbiage had the pidgin ring of science about it and made so little sense that Mort's ears refused entry to the words.

"All right. You're set. I've input the comm ID you gave me, and—"

"Good. If you're done, go have yourself a beer."

"I don't—"

"I don't care. You finished the job; quit fishing for approval. A job can be done perfectly and no one knows about it but you, and it doesn't change the fact that you performed superlatively. The praise of one technologically illiterate layman ought not to concern you."

Trebla looked up. He'd hung his head as he'd been harangued, but there was a new light in his eyes. "You used to tell me that."

"And you never listened."

"It didn't used to make sense. I think... maybe now I get it."

Mort harrumphed. "That shrinking violet of yours."

"Jas?"

"Yes, Jasmine. She works for you."

"It's not like that."

Mort waved away the implication that he objected to the relationship on workplace grounds or any other. "Point is, she toils in the intestines of this great tin can of a whale, right?"

"Sure. Mostly backbone stuff. Keeps out of sight."

"And if I told her she was a real crackerjack at her job? She'd take that as high praise?"

Trebla smirked. "Doubt it. A wizard commenting on engineering work?"

"Same goes for you. I'm not going to tell you you've done a good job. How the hell would I know? You just make sure that little girlfriend of yours knows *you* appreciate her work, same as I remark on Sparta's successes."

"Or Eric's?" Trebla joked.

Mort couldn't help wiping a hand over his face. "Soon as that one does something right, he'll be the first I'll tell. Now, shoo."

Trebla saluted, whapped the screen, and scurried out the door. By the time it had shut behind him, a little swirly pattern had sprung to life, hinting that the tech might be working properly...

... if Mort had wanted to talk to a swirling vortex of primary colors.

PLEASE WAIT

"What else do you expect me to do?"

PLEASE WAIT

"If I wasn't planning to wait, I wouldn't still be standing here, would I?"

PLEASE WAIT

Mort grumbled under his breath.

Before he did something he'd need to call Trebla back to fix, the panel connected him to Emperor Khosrau.

"So, you've made your decision?" the screen asked, and it might as well have been a mirror. Mort had worn that face long enough that he'd grown accustomed to it mimicking his every twitch and scowl.

But this was Emperor Khosrau Blackstone, the third incarnation—assuming the real Hadrian hadn't been fool enough to extract the nails from that book.

"I have."

"And your associates?"

"They'll play ball. No one likes the Martian color guard playing politics. And more than a passing few of them like Carl well enough to stick their neck out for him. We're in."

The smile that reflected back from the screen wasn't one Mort had used often—at least, not while he was gazing into a mirror. "Pardon me if I don't take you at your word."

"So pardoned."

"I'll need an oath."

"You'd be a fool not to want one."

"And you'll swear?"

"Depends on the wording."

"Naturally," the emperor replied. "You will kill General Bob Randall. You will also kill all the members of his inner circle, his assistants, his descendants, and the military government line of succession present on Mars. That will leave nominal leadership of the government in the hands of an Admiral Colleen Sherwin, currently in command of a fleet from her battleship, the *MNV Augustus*. She has two granddaughters and a niece in custody on Earth. Her, we can deal with to arrange a surrender."

"Not really hearing an oath in there."

"Your oath will be to carry out this plan without undue delay, deviation, or deception. You will be candid with me in all aspects of mutual intelligence sharing. You will not seek to seize power for yourself. In return, I guarantee the safety and comfort of Carl Ramsey in the interim and his release upon fulfillment of your oath."

Mort rubbed his smooth chin. "And your people will give us the support we need to make this happen? I can't just knock on a few doors and incinerate whoever answers. Well, I could, I suppose, but that wouldn't get the job done in this case."

"Yes. I'll be providing any information you'll need. This will be a top priority."

"Fine, then. I'll swear it."

"It's just the two of us. Use your true identity."

Part of full cooperation would probably entail revealing that Mort had informed the *Arete* crew already. This was less a deep, dark secret than Emperor Khosrau might have liked to think.

"I, Mordecai The Brown, do solemnly swear, upon my power, that I will abide by the terms of my agreement with Emperor Khosrau Blackstone, otherwise known as Hadrian The Brown. I will eliminate the Martian Military

Government's top officials, leaving some inconsequential nobody of an admiral in charge. And if Carl Ramsey is not released unharmed, unhindered, and unencumbered from his imprisonment, or if I have found him to be unduly mistreated during his captivity, I swear by the blood in my veins that I will avenge him.

"That good enough for you?"

It was so damnably impossible to read the nonsense going on with that face, that face he knew all too well, but which appeared now so alien to him. But it seemed that Khosrau found that blunt, no-nonsense oath something of a surprise.

"Indeed. I will put the appropriate people in contact with you to begin the preparation for this endeavor. I need not tell you that this matter demands the utmost secrecy. Tell no one you can't trust with that oath of yours."

"If you didn't need to tell me, you shouldn't have. Now, fuck off. I've got thinking to do."

The screen bulged and wrinkled and went blank as Mort clenched a fist. There was probably some proper, technological way to end the connection, but he didn't care to wait for help with it.

Heaving a sigh, Mort stared down at the inscribed circle on the floor around him, confirmed by the little chimp to be out of view of the camera. An angry purple glow faded as its protections against swearing oaths subsided.

It would be a cold day in the guild hall of the Order of Prometheus before someone pulled a fast one on Mordecai The Brown.

━━━

Far from the *Arete* and several hours offset from their chronos, another dinner assembled. This one, far more exclusive than

Captain Ramsey's, was a mere singular guest accompanied by the bare minimum of servants.

Emperor Khosrau Blackstone was not a man known for his exotic or refined palate. Hadrian hadn't needed to accustom himself to caviar and pate. And while, as emperor, he could have ordered the most expertly prepared fugu, he'd never found the idea of poisonous fish appealing in the first place.

Luckily, Khosrau's lone dinner companion was of even a less pretentious mien than his former life.

Carl Ramsey took huge bites of his Earth-raised steak burger, dolloped with ketchup, slathered with aerosol cheese, and stacked with bacon—nearly raw, at his request—and chatted as he chewed. "You might wanna consider something stronger than beer. Your hands are still shaking."

The damned spacer was a chameleon. Not a spy in Khosrau's employ wouldn't benefit from a few weeks under this one's tutelage and taking copious notes. Bartender. Folk musician. Doting father. He was all of these without so much as a hiccup. Starfighter pilot. Smuggler. War criminal. These all fit him as well—the latter convincingly portrayed by the eyndar spectacle, even if few within Earth Navy agreed with the characterization.

Tonight, among his many ancillary roles, Carl was playing the amiable prisoner.

There was a dissonance Khosrau had to keep in mind, every breath he took and every bite he chewed, that this affable dolt would turn him into a decorative fountain spouting his own blood if the opportunity arose for an escape.

Every word. Every action. Every unspoken thought, the man needed to be considered in that light. He'd do what it took, no matter what that entailed, in order to secure his own survival.

"A muscular tremor. Nothing more."

"Hey, at least those 'tremors' are only in your hands. Plenty of guys lose bladder control after a chat with Mort." He made casual small talk of bargaining with an elite assassin. That same intonation could just as easily have been used between two old men discussing their preferred dietary fiber supplement.

"You know him as well as anyone, I imagine. Do you suspect he'll find some loophole to worm his way out of our deal?"

"Nah. He doesn't need to. Plus, I doubt Mort really cares for those Martians in the first place. After all, when he had the job, they were a pain in his ass, too. Plus, it's a classic tale."

Khosrau paused in lifting a Nevrokopi potato chip to his lips. "Explain. Classic how?"

"A comeback story. Old heavyweight champ. Forced into retirement by age. Still feels like he's got something left in the old fuel rods. Some Faustian bargain gives him a fresh new body and a crack at an old rival he couldn't take down in his heyday. Story practically writes itself."

The chip crunched as Khosrau bit down, releasing a wave of flavors from imported peanut oil, Cornish sea salt, and the Nevrokopi potatoes themselves. "So, you think he'll do this gladly?"

"Oh, don't get me wrong, you're pissing him off to hell and back. You can drag a kid out for ice cream, but if you're dragging them, there's no amount of ice cream that'll stop them being pissed at you."

"I wonder if your experience in parenting was colored by raising Jessica as your eldest."

The spacer's laugh sounded so genuine that Khosrau almost believed they were having an amiable conversation. "Maybe. You hear about parents wishing that their kids have to raise a little copy of themselves someday. My old man was the galaxy's biggest asshole, but even *he* never wished *that* on me. Happens anyway, though."

"You do understand that the more you can help me manage him, the smoother this whole prisoner release will run. Don't you?"

"Emperor, old buddy, old pal o' mine. I just spent the longest week of my life getting shit on figuratively and pissed on literally by a bunch of speech-impaired pack hunters without a brain cell to share among them. Yet here I am, sitting with the emperor of the cosmos, eating one of the five or ten best burgers of my life and drinking a top-50 beer. What've I got to complain about?"

Oh, was that ever a loaded question. Being taken hostage. The implicit threat of death or torture if Mordecai The Brown didn't cooperate. The repeated deflections when Carl had hinted that he could entertain a few of the more neglected members of the ever-growing imperial harem, and if Khosrau made a threat of it, his wife couldn't get mad at him.

"You're right, of course. Care for dessert?"

———

Her duffel fuffed onto the bed, mussing a bedspread that probably cost more than many humans earned in a year. The chandelier swayed like a hangman's noose, high above. Probably wouldn't snap loose and crash down onto her in her sleep. Probably. Tiffany sighed and slipped out of her shoes, chastising herself for paranoia.

Plush rugs felt wonderful beneath bare feet. Chipped nail tint was an excuse to treat herself to a pedicure. Padding over to the window, savoring each step, she drew back the curtain and stared into the boundless Caledonian Ocean. Lit by external floodlights, a coral reef lazed past, teeming with colorful little fish.

"Bullshit assignment."

They'd taken away her ship. Something about necessary repairs, replacing permanently damaged parts that had seen too much astral travel, and valuing her personal safety. It had taken days to get here to her next job.

And they hadn't even told her what it would be.

Somewhere aboard the *Neptune's Reverie* was a contact who'd fill her in on the details. Whatever it was, the target had better be on the ship, too. Otherwise, there would be a two-week delay as Tiffany was cooped up with a bunch of rich, bored socialites, ne'er-do-wells, and retirees.

There was a knock at her cabin door.

Only two kinds of people existed in the galaxy: ones that were trying to kill her and ones that weren't. Both had reason to knock.

Poised to strike first, if need be, Tiffany pressed herself to the wall beside the door as she triggered the release.

Lifting her head away from the wall, she found a smiling bellhop.

"Wizard Tiffany, may I enter?"

Relaxing a hair, Tiffany stepped into the doorway before moving aside to allow passage. "Come on in. What is it?"

The door slid shut. The bellhop's smile shone. "Wizard Tiffany, you were promised a contact and assignment by your superiors on Earth."

"Associates," Tiffany clarified. She didn't care whether he was referring to Azrael, Emperor Noodledick, or just the Convocation in general. None of them were "superior" to her. "What've you got for me?"

"Your assignment is to remain aboard the *Neptune's Reverie* for the duration of this cruise and avail yourself of any amenities you wish, on the condition that you return to Earth relaxed, sated, and in good spirits."

"You're fucking kidding me! I'm on vacation?"

"No need to sound distraught."

"I could have vacationed on Earth. Parisian crepes for breakfast. Sushi from Ishikawa Prefecture for lunch. A Moroccan kickboxing instructor for dinner. I didn't need to traipse across a quarter of the galaxy to bob around in a reverse fishtank for three weeks to relax."

"It *does* sound as though the ship and view alone haven't done the trick," the bellhop agreed, his smile never faltering. "However, I am at your disposal for the entirety of the voyage to make this trip as enjoyable as possible in whatever manner you desire."

Tiffany folded her arms and shifted her weight to one foot. "Whatever manner, huh?" She glanced at his nametag and found it blank. In the process, she sized him up. Mid-twenties. Good posture. Probably worked out, but it was hard to tell with the uniform on. A shadow of stubble gave him a rakish air. Soft brown eyes invited Tiffany to swim in them. "What's your name, kid?"

"Anything you like."

It didn't take Tiffany three seconds to come up with one. "Raul work for you?" He didn't sound European at all, but that didn't particularly matter.

"As you wish, Wizard Tiffany."

She nodded approvingly, still not quite sure what she had and what it could do for her. "This a service the cruise line normally offers?"

"I don't work for the Caledonia Cruises or any of the other

tours. I'm a professional gentleman companion and loyal citizen of the empire. So long as I'm returned roughly in my present condition, you may do with me as you please for the duration of the cruise."

Closing the gap between them with two strides, Tiffany went button by button down the front of the bellhop uniform, revealing smooth-shaved pecs and abs. She ran her hands over them, checking for firmness and texture, then sliding them up and under the shoulders of the uniform jacket and lifting it off him.

Without forewarning, she hopped up, wrapped her arms around his neck, and turned her hips. Raul caught and cradled Tiffany in his arms.

"Take me up to the sunbathing deck. Let's go lie back, watch dolphins fuck in the sky overhead, and get a mood on. You strike me as a beer man, but my Raul likes gin and tonic with a little umbrella in his, I think. After that, we'll head back here and see what happens. Fair warning, I'm not shy about how I got my scars, but if you ask, you might hear shit that'll haunt you forever, got it?"

The ship bounced with Raul's gait as he carried Tiffany out the door. "Whatever you like."

Maybe this vacation wouldn't be so bad after all. Other than work, she didn't get off Earth often these days.

⊏⊐

"This is crazy, right? I can't be the only one here who thinks this is crazy."

Trebla glanced around the Briefing Room table in search of support for his position. But the others didn't seem concerned. Portable holo-projectors supplemented the room's main system, resulting in a museum-like array of planetary views, a boardroom's worth of graphs, and a cavalcade of headshots belonging to Martian leaders.

"Oh, just shut up and plot the destruction of a corrupt military aristocracy," Lisa told him without looking up from a datapad she referenced.

"But I thought we weren't going to be doing that?"

Jessie set down a datapad of her own. "Look, I know this is complicated, but we need to give every appearance that we're playing along with Khosrau's plan for Mars. That means being ready with answers to dumb questions we'd *have* to know if we were putting any effort in on our end. And it'll all look a *fuckload* more suspicious if we act all incredulous any time anyone brings up the Martian coup plan."

"Sorry."

"IT IS ALL RIGHT. I, TOO, FIND THE PROSPECT OF CHANGING A GOVERNMENT BY FORCE TO BE DIFFICULT TO INGEST."

"Swallow," Jessie corrected without pausing in her research.

Daphne stopped the parade of faces. "I think we've got a census of all the officials who'd need to be removed in order to break the command structure."

Trebla snatched a copy on his datapad and scanned through as the others watched Daphne present her final list.

Crazy. Absolutely nutso. There were nearly a hundred names. "Hadrian—I mean, Mort—are you seriously OK with this?"

The wizard glanced up from a clipboard, where a scrap of parchment accepted abuse from a ratty bird feather dipped in ink. "Huh? Oh, sure. Why not? We're not *doing* it, so what's it matter if it's a helluva lot of work?"

"No. I mean... like who's going to buy that we can pull this all off?"

"Everyone," Mort assured him.

Jessie nodded. "You didn't see him on the eyndar homeworld. It was something else."

"Nothing against Uncle Carl, but... like... 94 guys?" He leaned back in his seat and lifted all four hands, palm up. "Seriously? That's a lot of blood to spill."

Mort set down his clipboard and left the quill hanging in midair. "Look here. I don't leave bloody messes. It's one thing if you're looking for the shock value in a killing, but enjoying the sight of blood for its own sake is a sign of derangement. I barely leave ash anymore. I"—he sat up taller in his chair—"am a professional."

"Forget the blood!" Trebla protested. "Isn't 94 dead guys an awfully big price to pay?"

"Not really."

"We probably killed more on Outpost 71," Lisa pointed out.

"And Ghenlar Par'Mol."

Trebla malfunctioned. "I, uh. Yeah, all right. But—but this isn't like that."

"How?"

"It's just that... I mean..."

"They were just eyndar," Jessie suggested. "And these are humans."

"I'M not human!" How many times did this have to come up? And this wasn't about Jasmine, either, and he'd fight anyone who tried to claim otherwise.

Mort grunted. "Whatever. Human. Laaku. All descended from the same chimps."

Trebla saw red. Next thing he knew he was atop the Briefing

Room table, wading through holographic fields and marching his way up to the impertinent wizard's chair. "I am NOT descended from chimps. Mom and Dad always said to let it slide. Hell, I think Dad probably even *believes* it. But humans and laaku aren't evolved from the same species! No two races from the Gallery of Life are!"

Mort calmly scanned up and down him. "Look like a chimp to me."

"Bonobo!" Trebla countered. "Similar. Closely related. NOT. CHIMPS."

The wizard studied Trebla all the more closely. "Hmph."

"Is that all you've got? A 'hmph'?"

"Learned something new today. Kudos. Doesn't happen as often as it used to. Used to think that old saying about old dogs and new tricks meant that you stop being able to learn when you got older. I've come to realize that it's more that you know damn near everything by a certain point."

Trebla couldn't believe his ears. "You're just..."

"Yeah. New information. Love it. Four score years touring this spilled-sugar star cluster, and that's the first I'm hearing of this. No reason to doubt you, but I'll verify it later in case you're the one who's been misinformed."

Charlotte chose that moment to enter the Briefing Room, only head and shoulders as she leaned. "It's time. Captain. Commodore. Wizard Mordecai. Emperor Khosrau's people should be on the comm shortly."

"Time to go," Mort stated cheerily to the group as he slapped his thighs and stood. "Don't go plotting any stray coups while I'm gone. If we're conquering Bonobo Prime, I want in on the ground floor."

And just like that, Mort headed off with Jessie and Grosstet trailing in his wake.

He'd really wanted to be mad at the old bastard, but Trebla just couldn't manage any longer.

Jessie stood front and center as the comm connected. To her left, Mordecai The Brown glowered at the screen. To her right, Grosstet took up the remainder of the camera.

When Khosrau appeared, his first reaction was surprise. "I hadn't expected you to be taking the lead."

"Update your expectations." She tilted her head in Mort's direction. "This one's more of a fill-in-the-cracks-with-ash type of planner. I'm going to get this shit done."

"And Ambassador Grosstet?"

"THE HAATHEE PEOPLE SUPPORT THE SAFE RETURN OF CARL RAMSEY."

"Who are they?" Jessie demanded, and there was no questioning whom she meant. Like Mort, Khosrau had brought two advisers along. One was a shrewd-eyed wizard in house robes, indicating either quite a low station or quite a high one. The lack of ostentation was glaring beside the emperor's opulent regalia. The other, Jessie felt as if she ought to have known, but she hadn't made a study of Earth Navy admirals.

"This is Wizard Vincente, vizier to the emperor." The older wizard bowed his head in acknowledgment. "And Fleet Admiral Rodney Jessup, my chief military adviser."

OK. That was a name Jessie knew, at least. He'd been promoted during her five missing years, but despite never having met the man, he was a known quantity. Boring. Hard-nosed. By-the-book. No one who'd spoken to him would have admitted to *liking* the man, but he hoarded grudging respect like a miser.

"How much can we say in front of Old Rodeo?" Mort inquired with cold calculation.

"He knows. An unfortunate necessity. I can't have you holding that secret over me with my own people."

The admiral spoke up for himself. "I was, needless to say, distressed at this development."

"Oh, stuff a sock in it. If you'd done your job and brought Eric and Jessie safely to Earth, half of this wouldn't have happened. I've met cork boards that could hold up a rack of medals better than you, and it would fail all the same tasks you were assigned with less whining about them."

The admiral turned to Emperor Khosrau. There was no pretense of respect or deference. "If he'd wanted a free Mars under imperial control, he could have done this years ago!"

"We've all seen the Eyndar Empire," Khosrau countered before returning his attention to the *Arete* side of the conversation. "You wouldn't have any way to know, but the situation among the eyndar is dire. The opening salvos of a civil war have already been exchanged in the Black Ocean. On their homeworld, assassinations and arrests are rampant. And it was all due to one wizard lighting the right fire in the right place at the right time, purely by accident. We intend to do better. A clean coup. No blood. A little ash. A return to normalcy for the Martian people after years of rebellion and dictatorship."

"Good sales pitch," Jessie remarked deadpan. "Be nice if I believed it was altruism. But right now, I don't care."

Vincente raised his chin. "Pragmatism will serve us all quite well. I have been working with the Convocation to put together a team to assist you on the ground on Mars. This need not be some grand, heroic solo crusade. Success demands the proper resources, vetted, tested, and understanding that the only factor paramount to toppling the Martian regime is the secrecy of the effort. If our role is revealed, we'll cause even greater chaos with no moral high ground to—"

"Zip it, you glorified newspaper courier," Mort snapped. "We don't need you explaining how this works."

"I ENJOY THE THEATER OF THE MOOT," Grosstet protested.

Mort grunted. "Fine. I'll fill you in over beers, later. Just know that I may have sworn an oath that'll protect your sorry asses, but until Carl's having one right along with us, I'm keeping my options open for revenge."

Sensing that he was looking for a straight man for this comedy routine, Jessie helpfully jumped in. This was an old Uncle Enzio bit. In olden days, helpful comedic partners could expect ice cream next time they visited civilization. "Any good candidates?"

The wizard raised one eyebrow. "Yeah. Binding his soul in a book's too good for a double-crosser. I was thinking trapping him in a smutty magazine and leaving him in the washroom of a fertility clinic."

Jessie couldn't suppress a chill.

Khosrau's glare burned hot enough to ward off an actual shiver. "I'll keep my end of the bargain. Mind yours. There are over three months to the Martian elections. The pretense of freedom will only serve to cement the usurpers' hold. I'd like this matter resolved prior to November."

"I assume you have plans for how to get Hadrian here to Mars without raising flags?" Jessie stated the question but made it clear she expected an answer.

The emperor smiled, and Jessie imagined she saw the real Hadrian The Brown in that moment. "I really think that's a problem you can best solve on your own. Do not attempt to contact us."

The screen went dark.

Jessie studied the wizard. "Is there a solid reason why everyone in your family is a raging asshole?"

Mort just shrugged and headed for the cabinet where he kept the tumblers. "What can I say?"

"You think you've got it in you to be this?" Jessie asked, hooking a thumb the impostor Hadrian's way.

Eric, who'd been silent as a mouse, sitting in a corner the cameras couldn't see, nodded.

"You can talk now."

"Oh. Right. Sure. I knew that. Yeah. I think I can be Mort. I mean, I know Mort as well as anyone. Well, not like Sparta knows him or Dad knows him, but I've got my own way and I think I know him well enough that I can fool anyone who doesn't *really* know any better."

"Try me," Jessie challenged.

Mort watched with idle curiosity while pouring a glass of whiskey.

Eric cleared his throat. "Harrumphity dumfle-dumpf. I'm going to incinerate all you nincompoops. Fix my holo-projector so I can drink beer and watch a documentary about salad dressing because it's named after a Roman guy."

Jessie couldn't even muster the humor to appreciate the effort on a sarcastic level because it appeared that Eric was perfectly sincere. "Oh. Dead ringer."

Mort threw back a shot and handed the rest of the bottle to Grosstet, who did likewise. "We'll work on it."

It was three days later that the intel dump arrived.

The holovid theater became the War Room, with the main projector partitioned and diverted via splitters into numerous workstations. Grosstet and Trebla had isolated the computers via a monitored link that allowed data to pool in an eddy within the data storage system but not escape.

Last thing anyone around the *Arete* needed was Earth Navy Intelligence installing software without authorization.

To their credit, Earth's preeminent military organization had been remarkably forthcoming with their sharing. While the *Arete* had once been able to crack the organization's codes with ease, it seemed suspicious that *someone* might have clued them in to change their encryption more often. Plus, getting it freely delivered reduced the chances that any given piece of intel was planted as a trap for anyone with improper access to use to their own detriment.

For now, that factor was out of play, and Jessie wasn't even the chief player. That honor belonged to the youngest member of the crew.

"Captain!" Daphne called out upon seeing Jessie enter the War Room. The azrin rushed over, out of uniform, wearing jogging pants and a hooded sweatshirt with the sleeves cut off. All of that, Jessie had been fully prepared to overlook, but then she noticed her security officer was also barefoot.

"Taking a casual approach?" she teased.

Daphne followed her captain's gaze to the floor. "Oops. Sorry, ma'am. I've been sleeping in the seats, and this is more comfortable than a uniform as far as pajamas go. But I can run back to my—"

"As you were, Lieutenant," Jessie cut in, letting the matter drop. "What've we got so far?"

"The biggest win we've discovered is calendar snaps for most of the major players." She flicked a finger over her datapad, and a section of the holo field shifted. A wireframe cityscape vanished, replaced by a grid of dates and the name of someone Jessie didn't recognize, marking him as someone low down the priority list of kills.

Appearances. Appointments. Meetings. Recurring duties.

"Why is some of that stuff showing gray?" Jessie asked, aiming a finger overhead into the mix.

"Observations and habits. Earth Navy has people on Mars

feeding this stuff back via secure channels. For instance, Commander Haversham here eats at the same deli every Tuesday and takes his morning jog at 0515 hours."

The implications were staggering. "You've got this for all 94 names on our list?"

Daphne shrugged. "This is one of the better caches— Marcus Haversham is a creature of habit—but yeah. To one degree or another, we've got intel like this on everyone."

"Great."

"Almost a shame we're not actually freeing Mars from these tyrants. Some of the stuff in these intel packages really doesn't paint these guys in a flattering light."

What would hers show? Jessie had accessed her own personnel file despite being on the outside of the classified data file window. But what would an intelligence agency have on her? Nothing flattering to *her*, that much was certain. "Cut them some slack. It's coming from people who want them dead. Don't expect journalistic integrity. And try to stop mentioning the ruse. We're going to be saddled with a liaison before long, and then it's game on. No more slipups. Start getting used to it."

Daphne saluted. "Yes, ma'am."

"Now, show me how you plan on turning this intel dump into a mass murder."

"Do you have to put it like that?"

"Coup?"

"Better." Daphne let out a long breath. "All right. Let me show you what I've started working on."

The calendar from Commander Marcus Haversham winked out, and the wireframe cityscape from before appeared once again. No expert in Martian geography, one slice of the megalopolis looked the same as another.

Lines appeared, one by one, rapid-fire. Each was a trail of

little segments, joined by dots, each a different color from all the other lines, if only by slight shades in some cases. The lines zigzagged and crisscrossed and ran to and fro all over the map, occasionally disappearing off the map's extent entirely.

"This is the beginnings of a plan."

"What am I looking at?"

"A combined itinerary of all our targets," Daphne explained. She tapped and slid a finger along the surface of her datapad. The lines resolved into single dots. As her finger moved, the dots hopped all over. "I can show you the projected locations for all our targets at any date and time from now until the Martian elections."

"Lotta work for someone to run these guys all down before their security teams realize what's going on and whisk them off to what remains of 94 safe houses."

"We're working on a solution to that," Daphne promised.

"Sleep in a bed tonight, Lieutenant," Jessie ordered in reply.

"Yes, ma'am."

There was keeping up a ruse and there was obsessing over a ruse. Jessie swore that she would keep her crew on the right side of that equation, even if it wasn't going to be her *running* the ruse for much longer.

———

"Mort" schlepped through the corridors of the *Arete* as if he'd hardly been down most of them before. He gawked at the frequent haathee artwork, trying to fathom the minds that created these vistas and what spots on Earth they might have represented. Each techno-gadget got the stink-eye. But it was the people who interested him on these jaunts.

Trebla crawled out from inside a panel like the galaxy's

worst stage magician, huffing and pushing a satchel of tools ahead of him. He grinned when he spotted the wizard, deepening his voice and calling out, "Yo, Hadrian!"

"Mort."

"Right. Sorry. I don't have an ancient flatvid for that one. What brings you down to Comm Relay Node 17 this morning?"

The wizard gave a harrumph. "My feet."

"OK. I get it. *That* mood. I'll leave you alone to ruminate or cogitate or obfuscate. Whatever kind of skating you need, have at it."

A snicker and a whim struck simultaneously. With a flick of deft fingers, the floor frosted over with a glaze of sheer ice. With a push from the last bit of unfrozen steel, the wizard slid away down the hall, poised on one foot with his hands clasped at his back.

"This shit had better sublimate!" the laaku chief engineer shouted after him.

Further wandering brought him to the main kitchen, where the scent of mushroom soup lured him like an Achaean ship onto a siren's rocky shore.

"What's on the menu, young lady?" he asked, nose lifted, eyes heavy-lidded.

"Ha ha. Harmony's science. May have. Me feeling. More spry. But I. Have toenails. Older than. You. But to. Answer your. Question. Whatever you. Like. What is. *Currently.* Cooking is. Uumabi mushroom. Soup."

"Mort" rubbed his chin stubble. "Uumabi's roughly Keru's equivalent of Japan, if I'm not mistaken."

"Damned if. I. know. Geography of. Other. Keru-like. Planets was. Never something. That came. Up."

"Island chain. Off the coast of the Benbar Landmass." His own Keru geography was spotty at best.

"Sounds about. Right. Are you. Interested in. Lunch or. Are you. Just here. To inquire. About the. Smell?"

That was a good question. Was he hungry enough to eat? "I'll give the soup a while to stew. Might mosey on back once I'll be better able to appreciate it."

"Mort's" continued wanderings took him into more and more populated regions of the ship. He dodged a shift change outside the Logistics barracks, acknowledging the hardworking backbone of the ship's workforce with polite, if somewhat curt, nods and the mindful placement of each footstep.

A door opened, and Lorenzo exited. He made less eye contact than even a close crossing with a wizard warranted and didn't speak a word. Charlotte lingered at the doorway, watching her patient depart.

"I don't suppose *you've* come to book an appointment," Charlotte scolded, though he'd done nothing wrong.

The wizard shook his head. "Perish the thought. These young legs just demand a certain degree of stretching, and I'm still of a mind to indulge their whims."

Despite dressing in what could be best described as cozy-core-harmless, all soft wool and shapeless lines, she had a cold, hard edge in her voice. "Indulge them elsewhere, if you're able. You're a walking dispensary of emotional trauma, and you don't even *sound* like Hadrian. Keep to your circle of plotters and avoid spreading nightmares to the crew of this vessel."

"It's not *my* fault if Hadrian put his own voice to poor use. Give a mouse a megaphone, it still just squeaks. I, for one, appreciate the smooth baritone presently at my disposal."

"Good day."

Well, that was that. Charlotte didn't wish good days on anyone she wished to continue speaking with. Thus, with the shutting of a door between them, "Mort's" trek resumed.

He worked no magic. His hands remained casually tucked inside sleeves.

The *Arete* gurgled and hummed and clanked and whirred and chatted and puttered and bustled all around him as he made his way through the veins and arteries of the great scientific beast.

"There you are!" Sparta called out, coming up from behind him in a disused haathee lounge that had been half given over to Jomek's repair flotsam. But the other half remained available to impromptu relaxation for another willing to either do a touch of climbing or pretend that a footrest was meant for use by other than haathee feet. "I've been looking all over for you."

"I've been all over; didn't see you there."

Sparta scanned their environs with a disapproving look. "Not ideal, but it'll do."

"Do how?"

She folded her arms. "You agreed. I know it wasn't an oath, but I'm not having you back out on me at this point."

This could be a problem. What agreement did she mean? One of the best ways through any uncomfortable situation was to cede control and ride it out. "I'm not backing out."

Sparta looked different. Her smile was so relaxed, so easy. She swayed right up to him and stood on the ends of his shoes, craning on tiptoe as she wrapped her arms around his neck and kissed him. Tall as she was, Hadrian's body had inches to spare on her, and she knew all the tricks for making up the difference.

"I'm not letting you go off on another suicide mission without an honest attempt at getting pregnant first. And once or twice a day isn't going to cut it."

She had a constrictor's grip around him. He could feel the shape of her body through the flimsy chiffon of the sleeveless white A-line dress. Though mostly skin and bones, she squooshed against him. When Sparta kissed him again, she slid her tongue into his mouth.

What was there to do but...

... pull away and come clean.

"I'm sorry! I'm not Mort!"

"No kidding," Sparta replied with a smirk, wiping her lips with the back of a hand. "But the body is dead on." She backed away a step, scanning him up and down. "At least in looks."

"What did I do wrong? Even Charlotte didn't know I was me."

That drew a chuckle that jangled the little chains Sparta wore all over. "You didn't act like Eric. That much I'll give you. But you weren't quite Mort, either. You need more practice, and we've only got a few days until Earth Navy and the Convocation stick us with babysitters posing as official liaisons."

"Can you be more specific?"

"Mort looks at me with a hunger in his eyes. That was your first mistake. Also, he'd have been physically turned on by my advances."

Eric scowled with Hadrian's face. "I'm not sure I can mimic that."

Sparta took a seat on the footrest and patted a spot beside her, which Eric took her up on. "Look, they're liable to send someone who's familiar with one or both of us. I've got less acting to do than you, but we'll be sharing a bed and interacting in front of the crew."

"That's all we're doing in the bed, though. Just sharing. No snuggling," Eric warned.

Sparta sighed and leaned back, hooking her feet under the footrest to keep from toppling backward. "I wasn't lying about my deal with Mort. We have sex all the time, so I didn't think it would be that big a deal. But apparently remaining faithful to an estranged wife for fifty years, then taking over a body like *that*..." She paused to run a finger down the middle of Eric's torso, thankfully stopping in the vicinity of his belly button. "Well, I figure his wife Nancy must have had the libido of a panda or they'd have had a dozen kids."

"I really shouldn't be hearing all this, you know."

Sparta snorted. "You need to hear all this and more. You're getting superficial Mort. But you're not understanding him on a deeper level."

Eric squirmed in his borrowed body. "How deep are we talking?"

"Instincts. Feelings."

"Uncle Enzio—I mean, Mort—used to say that humans didn't have instincts. We're rational, even when we're irrational. And I don't think he has any feelings except smug and grumpy."

"You're doing an excellent grumpy and a decent smug, but there's more to him."

This still sounded worrisome. "How much more?"

"On our second date, he brought me lilies. I accused him of snooping into my life, but he claimed he'd noticed my eye straying to them as we passed a florist walking to dinner. He pays *attention* to things. Even at Oxford, most of the attention paid to me was smile and tits. Most of my dates and shitty, short-term boyfriends would have struggled to describe my eye color."

Eric couldn't see her eyes right now. She'd turned aside, possibly as a test. But he couldn't allow himself to fail one so easy. "Basically the color of Drippy's fur."

"Who or what is Drippy?"

"The dog from Lunchtime Letters." When he caught a scowl, he quickly added, "It's a compliment. Lovely shade and all."

Relenting with a laugh, Sparta draped an arm around Eric's shoulders. "By Athena's smile, you are going to be such a weird Mort while Mort's away."

━━━

Jessie relaxed in horse stance. It was an adaptation of kip-tie-mahl with her extensive hand-to-hand training prior to visiting Mortania. Master Bentho had drilled her on basics, and that had served her well, but even after perceived years of study, it never felt natural—or at least, a comfortable version of *super*natural. He was also fucking imaginary, so if he had any beef with how Jessie put his lessons into effect in the real world, he could go self-violate his imaginary vow of chastity.

By the time the *sproing-click* reached her ears, her hand was already moving. An apple-sized beanbag deflected harmlessly away from her face. Another *sproing-click*, and she was mid-whirl to kick another out of the air behind her.

Relaxing back into her wide, sturdy stance, she blocked out all extraneous noise.

The gym was sparse, but Jessie wasn't alone. Fleshy slaps against artificial wood and rhythmic thumps were Mindy working out on the Wing Chun dummy. By the mere sound of the footwork, she could tell the young security officer was still thinking her way through the routines rather than reinforcing instincts.

Sproing-click.

Another of the beanbag-lobbing machines fired, and Jessie backflipped, kicking the harmless projectile into the air. She landed in a handstand.

The gym door slid open.

Sproing-click.

As the last beanbag fell, Jessie pinwheeled in place, kicking the falling one into the next one just launched.

"I imagine that's somehow a productive use of your time?" Harmony called out.

From Jessie's vantage, the ship's chief medical officer hung by her feet from the ceiling. Not that gravity mattered, if one stopped thinking about it. Rather than start a conversation that way, Jessie dropped into a half somersault and sprang to her feet as the doctor sauntered in.

"It's called practice, and I—"

"I was addressing Lieutenant Sedgwick," Harmony snapped. She continued through the gym toward the sweating novice practitioner of the hand-to-hand arts. "You're presently nineteen minutes late for your appointment and not answering your datapad."

Mindy froze, pulled from the reverie of mystical focus by shock and embarrassment. "Oh, shite! Soz, Doc! Lemme towel off real quick and I'll—"

"Shower. I'll reschedule you for 1130 hours." Harmony then ignored her test subject and stalked over to Jessie. "As for you, this is really how you're preparing for a mission? You destroyed literal billions of marbits' worth of H-tech medical research and set back the advancement of humanity so you could perform acrobatic juggling tricks in a fight?"

Jessie cracked her neck. "What are you getting so bent out of shape about? We've been over this. My natural reflexes were already interfering with the drones."

"We could have suppressed that with the right combination of programming the drones and retraining your autonomic responses."

That just sounded like programming *her*, too. "Look, I'm already giving you leeway to conduct your sentient trials on my crew. Everyone else seems happy with their results. Don't power your thrusters against the landing pad. Take your numerous wins and leave me to get myself ready for the mission that matters."

"You could be damaging the other subjects' drones using magic in closer proximity to them."

"I wasn't messing with the damn spring-launchers Jomek rigged up. I thought implantables were supposedly more resilient."

"In theory. But you're also a complete amateur with this whole wizard business."

A pedantic finger shot up instantly. "I'm not a wizard." Mort had been crystal clear on that point.

"All the worse."

The gym doors slid open again, and a tinier version of Harmony entered. "Mommy!"

Turning, the doctor visibly fought back her scowl. "Hi, baby. What're you doing here?"

"Uom'pe is making pizzas for lunch. Can I have some?"

Poor kid was stuck on a super specific nutrient regimen from the machine in the saloon. If Jessie had asked her parents for pizza at that age, Dad's only question would have been, "Is it free?"

"Do you have an ingredients list?"

Xrista shook her head, sending untamed hair flouncing. "Uh-uh. But Big Mommy said she'd make sure to get it from Uom'pe if you said yes."

Offering a melodramatic sigh of defeat, Harmony relented. "OK. But no more than two slices."

"Thanks, Mommy!" Xrista turned and raced off with a huge grin on her face. The door closed behind her.

"I used to get hugs every time she tracked me down shipboard."

But that wasn't what Jessie was wondering about. "Big Mommy?"

"Medic Daschel," Harmony clarified. "She's been spending more time around Xrista of late."

"Uh... huh..."

"Maintain your distance from the H-tech trial subjects while performing experimental, unsupervised magic, if you please, Captain," Harmony replied coolly. She turned to depart without seeking dismissal.

"Sure thing," Jessie called after her, unable to resist a parting barb, "Little Mommy."

⸻

"MY SHIP WILL BECOME A BATTLEFIELD YET AGAIN," Grosstet mused, seated on a mattress-sized cushion in the hookah lounge with a stein of beer in hand.

"Not if all goes to plan," Mort pointed out, taking a drink from his own pint glass. With Eric meandering the ship in his guise, it was as good a time as any for some day drinking and engaging with two of the few minds aboard worth polling for opinions.

"Plans are the coping mechanism for a galaxy that is fundamentally an arena of chaos." While not partaking in the booze, naturally, Figarus clutched the business end of a hookah pipe in one lower hand. He lounged on his back, sideways across a hammock, head back to view them all upside down.

Mort harrumphed. "I put the chaos in. I take it back out. It's all nice and tidy."

"I HAVE WANTED TO ASK, BUT THE SITUATION HAS NEVER ARISEN FOR IT TO BE POLITE. HOWEVER, YOU ARE NOT THE ORIGINAL HADRIAN."

"Yeah. The former occupant was a spineless little weasel who squandered what he had in pursuit of what he hadn't earned."

Figarus blew a smoke ring, then a plume that whooshed through it. "You give a man a fish, he ends up with fish breath. Give a man an empire, and he—"

"Triples the size of his harem the first month on the job," Mort cut in snidely. "I should have just made Vincente emperor and taken the boy's body by force."

"THAT SEEMS UN-HERDLIKE."

"You bet it is. Humans aren't herd animals. We're clannish. Only way to organize more than a few dozen of us is by force, explicit or otherwise. Laws are backed by police, military, inquisitors. Any law without force behind it is a suggestion. Governments last until a coup and stay in power by crushing anyone plotting one."

Grosstet swung his trunk back and forth, a sign of annoyance from what Mort had gathered. "I HAVE SEEN GOOD AND BAD FROM HUMANS, BUT THAT SOUNDS AS IF ALL THE GOOD IS PERILOUSLY CLOSE TO SUCCUMBING TO VIOLENCE AND EVIL."

Once more, Figarus had his own wacky opinions on the matter. "Good can only persist through the application of violence. However, violence is inherently evil."

Mort scoffed.

"You can't look behind yourself in a mirror."

"Philosophical laaku poppycock."

"A NEW WORD!" Grosstet immediately pulled out a datapad the size of a restaurant menu.

"It's an archaic form of bullshit," Figarus supplied helpfully. "Just like wizards. Thinkity-think-think-*boom*. Wizards can turn planets into worlds, but they spend most of their time blowing one another up and burrowing into minds where they don't belong."

"Most can't light their own farts on fire," Mort countered. "And you'd be shocked to discover how many die trying."

"DID YOU NOT LIKE BEING EMPEROR?"

Mort scowled and floated his glass over to the keg for a refill, which the haathee readily obliged. "Parts of it, sure. Getting your way to your face and having vermin all work behind your back to undo it all gets tiresome, though."

"The harem sounds like quite a perk to give up. Must have been hard."

"IT WAS! I HAVE HAD SIXTEEN MATES, THOUGH NEVER MORE THAN FIVE AT ONCE."

"He meant me," Mort chimed in. "You'd be surprised. I'd take one good woman over a gaggle of backstabbing social climbers. And to prove it, I did."

Figarus shook his head. "Father heirs. Stabilize a corrupt economic oligarchy. Divest from an unjust intergalactic hegemony. You could have done so much good with so little effort."

"Didn't take the job to do good. Took it to piss in the cornflakes of the traitors who murdered my wife in their coup. Settled a lot of old scores. Took care of the vengeance aspect. After that, it just became a parade of cosmic-scale chores and listening to the squabbling of petty opportunists. Kid was welcome to it up until he kidnapped Carl."

"JESSICA'S FATHER SEEMS UNIQUELY ABLE TO BOTH FIND AND ESCAPE TROUBLE."

"He's an addict. The next time he leaves well enough alone will be the first. And he possesses a gambler's optimism that ought to have gotten more people killed over the years than it actually has—well, at least, the people anyone cared about."

"YOUR DOING?" the haathee inquired.

Behind that prehensile snorkel and between those doormat ears lay a brain worth a damn.

"Statistics don't tell stories. Stories are the manure of selection bias."

Jury was out on whether the same could be said of the chemically impaired laaku.

"I scribble in the margins of the Grim Reaper's shopping list, sure," Mort answered with a shrug. "Plenty of times it's less a matter of preventing tragedies and more about assigning ownership to someone else."

"FIGARUS, IN REFERENCE TO OUR CONVERSATION ON THE NATURE OF EVIL IN HUMANS..."

The index finger of a free hand already aimed Mort's way. "This guy, right here. We've literally got the crew plotting him a mass murder."

"BUT... I LIKE HIM. DOES THAT MAKE ME EVIL AS WELL?"

"Nah," Figarus assured the haathee. "That's not how it works."

"IS IT ALL RIGHT THAT I CONSIDER HIM A FRIEND?"

Mort lifted his beer in a toast. "Better than being my enemy."

━━━

Meanwhile... on Mars...

Supreme General Robert "Bob" Randall leaned back and smoked a cigar as a corporal from his personal detail filed his toenails. After a career spent on his feet, this pedicure business was an indulgence he'd never considered until political realities thrust luxury into his lap.

"The situation in the Eyndar Empire continues to deteriorate. The Pine Fang Pack has declared no confidence in the new emperor, joining the Shallow Moon and Howling Star Packs in defiance of the imperial mandate."

"Animals, the lot of them," General Bob grumbled. He liked the moniker his campaign had come up with to make his hardline political stances appeal to the everyday Martian grocery shopper. There was more to him, as a father, a grandfather, and fifty-year veteran of the Marine Corps, than pacifying hostile territory. He was a fisherman, a painter (mostly of landscapes where he fished), a connoisseur of fine cigars. That was General Bob to his mind and to the minds of 49.3 percent of the voting public.

If only 0.8 percent could have yanked their bleeding-heart heads out of their asses to vote properly, none of this would have had to happen.

Colonel Kent nodded. "Yes, sir. Fortunately, none of the fighting has endangered human settlements thus far. However, a number of Earth-aligned border colonies are currently on high alert given how close the civil war battle lines are being drawn."

"Earth. Mars. Doesn't matter. Civilians are civilians. Humans are humans. Until they put on a uniform, they're just our people on the wrong side of a fence."

"Of course, sir. I didn't mean to imply otherwise. Only that it's not impacting our sphere of influence."

"It will. That house of cards over on Earth is going to topple sooner or later. They'll fall apart, and we'll have to pick up the pieces. Maybe it'll be our own people. Maybe we'll be ordering Earth Navy admirals around, but someone's going to have to go out there and put on a show of force to let the eyndar know their squabble's got no place in human space."

God dammit, he even talked in little rhyming sound bites

these days. Those nagging campaign advisers had permanently damaged his ability to communicate like a grown-ass man, let alone the supreme general of a multi-planet alliance.

"Right, sir. We've got MNN coming in for a one-on-one at 1300 hours. Domestic briefings at 1400. At 1600 hours, we have Mrs. Randall. Then, at 1610, you'll be in debate prep."

"We have an opponent for me, yet?" General Bob asked. "I don't like the idea of getting on that debate stage with a single podium. Bad look."

"Still working on that, sir. We're dragging the middle ground between your ardent supporters and avowed traitors, but it's a narrow field. Most of the plausible candidates swear they're one hundred percent behind you. No one wants to come out as the face of the opposition."

The supreme general chewed the end of his cigar. "Well, do what you have to. I'd say to guarantee the lamb's safety, but he's sacrificial for a reason." Thoughts percolated like field-ration coffee. "Hmm, maybe we set up a pipeline to the League. You know, exile. Give us some spit and polish after a bloody road getting where we are."

"Maybe we could float the exile proposal in advance of the debates. Have them remote, already in League space."

General Bob shook his head. "Naw. Need the handshake or it's not a real debate. Not every bastard's going to be a wizard who breaks three bones before letting go." He winced at the memory of that. Brilliant ploy, he had to admit. Wisp of a woman giving away 30 kilos to him, sneaks in a bit of magic that doesn't even flicker the stage lights or blur the holo feed. But the swelling and throbbing in that hand kept his signature gesticulating to a minimum and threw off his repartee.

"Understood, sir. I'll make sure the campaign team is—"

Inspiration had knocked. The general put up a hand to silence his deputy. "What about you?"

"Me, sir?" Kent squeaked.

"Think about it. Old versus young. Same vision for Mars. Let the voters decide whether my time has come. Legacy lives on, either way. Policies won't change. Everything else, you back me up on full-throat."

"But they'll kill me!"

"Exile. We'll make sure you have a security detail in place. You'll be doing Mars a favor, son."

"If I can find you a viable candidate before next Thursday evening at 2100 hours, am I off the hook, sir?"

General Bob gave the grandfatherly grin that gleamed at the end of every one of his adverts and on all his campaign posters and signs. "That sounds like a *fiiiine* plan."

One of the perks of being emperor was that everyone did what you said, at least in your presence. Khosrau had grown to hate holo-projectors. With live theater at his beck and call, orchestras available on a whim, and the Order of Morpheus on standby, he found little need for the technological devices any longer.

Illusion was just as good as science. Better, if the wizard in control had any artistic flair.

Wizard Ziyu had such a flair.

As an assemblage of dinner guests ate, she provided a view of Mars that was utterly stunning. It shone red where nature still held sway and glittered with cities over the rest of the planetary surface. Ships and orbital outposts lazed around. And, at the outskirts of the palace dining hall, Phobos and Deimos orbited.

Khosrau wagged a bite of rare steak, skewered on the end of his fork. "Now, you see, if we want to secure long-term control, we need to rein in any remaining resistance among the local magical population. I'm talking fealty oaths, tattooed loyalty runes, the works. And there will have to be public executions of the ringleaders. Anyone who even takes a sniff at the seat of power gets his head deposited in a jar. Last thing we need is the Martian Circle thinking that wizards can rule Mars."

There were chuckles around the table. Boss laughs, he knew. Especially since he hadn't been joking, though upon reflection, he could see how his statement carried more than a mere whiff of irony.

"We'll need a sizable purge of the fleet command structure, as well," Vincente pointed out. "But we ought to prefer demotions and forced retirements over executions." Every ruler needed a wet blanket like him. Obviously, if captains and admirals commanding Mars Navy's impressive fleets knew they were returning to Mars to see their heads and bodies delivered to separate addresses, there would be more than a few who mutinied on the spot.

"Right. Naturally. Fealty oaths there, too." Maybe the officers of Mars Navy wouldn't be as bound spirit and soul by such an oath, but they didn't need to know that.

Other advisers had their say as well, and Khosrau took note of them all.

"We ought to seize MNN with all their executives and on-air personalities. Get them to start putting out public notifications written by our people."

"I think a freeze on Martian banks... any account over ten million Marbits, at any rate."

"To hell with marbits. Declare them illegal currency. Grace period to exchange for terras at a steep discount."

"We need to get rid of their war memorials."

"And the statues."

"And ban the playing of that planetary anthem."

"Arrest the songwriter! Who was it? Jodi MacElmore?"

"She did *Soul of Mars* during the riots. No, it was Kenjamin Linus who wrote *Behind the Red Curtain*."

"Off 'em both! Bloody traitors."

This was where the calm, measured voice of reason had to step in. "What are you idiots talking about? We're bringing humanity *home* on Mars, not occupying an enemy planet. We'll issue subpoenas, make plea deals, suspend sentences. Make it look like these people are filthy criminals that get off easy thanks to our mercy. Mars is too vast to hold by force. We need the Martians on *our* side."

The new head of the Inquisition scoffed. "After we kill all their political leaders? How do you expect to pull *that* off?"

Khosrau dabbed at the corners of his mouth with a napkin. "Oh, I have a plan in the works."

Something had been nagging at her neurons, sneaking in between thoughts or training and preparation to inject doubt and worry where neither was helpful. It had helped focusing on her still-newfound magical abilities, but once Jessie hit the showers, she was trapped alone with no ready distractions.

She skipped the dryer in favor of a quick toweling off before dressing and heading out into the greater *Arete* in search of an end to the madness. It didn't matter which of the two she found first. But somewhere around the ship, there was a gangly, haughty young wizard who was getting a dose of reality from his captain.

It was in the saloon where Jessie found one of them. Hadrian's body. A beer. Crusty old Dad music likely on the PA system at his request.

"You. We need to talk."

"Me?" the wizard inquired, gesturing toward himself with a half-empty beer.

Oh, if Eric was the one drinking, he was in for *two* dressings-down. But Jessie had her own suspicions.

"Yes, you. And not here. Come with me."

"Sure thing," the Hadrian body replied.

The hallway outside the Soundcheck Saloon was good enough for now. Once the doors shut, the music ceased. An annoying, childish portion of her brain found irony that the doors were blocking out the band *The Doors*, but she brushed that thought aside.

"Which of you are you?"

"It's me," Hadrian's voice replied unhelpfully.

"Not funny."

"Fair. I suppose I don't look much like me, but I'm me'er than I've me'd in a long, long while. And if you're struggling to tell, that's all the more evidence that he can pull this off."

"So, then, you're the Mort who was Uncle Enzio?"

"Like I said... I'm me." There was a glint of mischief in those old eyes that Jessie didn't quite dare look into too closely. If Eric was that good, maybe she didn't have to worry.

But she didn't believe it for a second.

"We need a new plan. Eric's walking into a death trap. Even if he pulls off the impersonation, the first time he's challenged—really challenged—he's going to crumple because he's *not you*."

"Plan doesn't need him to be. All setup. No third act. Not even a first intermission if it goes off without a hitch—not that they ever do."

Jessie gritted her teeth. "That's the problem. If things *do* go off plan, Eric's not equipped to solve messy, gory problems the way you are. If our half goes sideways, we'll muddle through it—"

"Granted."

"—but Eric's bound to just fumble around, make things worse for himself and everyone else, and resort to some kind of crazy chronomancy."

"He *does* have something of a habit," Mort admitted. "But a bunch of Martians showing back up in time for the next flyby of Halley's Comet isn't a bad thing, either."

"You say that, but it's just as likely that one of these times, someone's going to corner Eric and overpower him. Tiffany's done it. You can do it. I can't believe that in the whole of the Convocation—or whatever-the-fuck the Martians are calling theirs these days—there aren't others."

"You know what you need?" Mort reached out and Jessie froze. But all he did was lift a lock of sopping-wet hair. It was long enough by now that it draped limply over one finger as Mort withdrew. "Fewer showers."

"Excuse me?"

"You heard me. You always had this problem. Do. Do. DO. Then, all sweaty and worked up, you get into the shower and go off *thinking*. And, frankly, you're a mess at it."

"Since when!" It was less a question than an accusation. Jessie did some of her best reflecting in the shower. It was isolating. Earth Navy had gotten her into the habit of a quick, scalding rinse, but once she graduated to special forces, it was either on assignment with no access to running water and spare time or free rein to use her off-duty hours as she pleased. A long, soaking shower was a salve to both mind and body.

"Since you started taking long showers to get peace and quiet from the *Mobius* denizens. Mostly harmless, I grant you, but most of your half-cocked worries came from the showerhead."

"Name one."

OK. That was probably a mistake. Knew it as soon as she

said it, but now the words were out there, and she'd given a wizard—*this* wizard—a pathetically low hurdle to clear.

"Joining Earth Navy despite the significant negative examples provided by damn near every adult in your life."

"That wasn't a mistake," she insisted.

"What about the time when you ended your friendship with Chrystal Park after a good, wet think?"

Jessie huffed. Not this old shit again. "We were leaving Odiorne VI anyway, and I was pretty sure she was starting to think we were more than friends. It was for her own good."

"Every time you two got drunk on half a beer apiece, you couldn't keep your hands off one another. Don't know *where* she got that idea."

That brought a scowl unbidden. "I don't remember that."

"Since you didn't stop at that half beer, usually, I'm not surprised. But it just proves my point that you're an irresponsible shower planner. No one to ask for advice. No gizmos to look up facts. You turn into a know-nothing know-it-all and work yourself up into a tizzy."

"I do *not* get myself worked up. And not over nothing."

"You are presently in such a state, my dear."

That snapped a rubber band that had been holding the gears in her brain from turning. "Don't give me that 'my dear' bullshit. I'm not ten anymore and you're not... however-the-fuck-old Uncle Enzio supposedly was. And I'm right about Eric. He's *not* ready for this. I'm not trading a brother for a father!"

Mort snickered. "Well, you do have *two* brothers and only the one father." He must have realized that Jessie's deepening scowl was too serious for making light of the situation, as he hastily amended, "But we're not sacrificing Eric. He'll be a distraction. It's a role he's damn good at. And no one involved from Earth's side of things will know either of us well enough personally to tell the difference. I heard he slipped one past Charlotte, even."

"He did?" Jessie's brain fired thrust reversers.

"Yup. Don't underestimate your little brother. He's not so little anymore. And he's more of a wizard than those pointy-headed Convocation worrywarts give him credit for."

"He fooled Charlotte?" That woman understood her brother better than anyone ever had. He was happy around her, not an amiable sort of lost. And she kept him on task, behaving mostly appropriately in public, and dressing like a respectable member of the crew. To think that she could be taken in by a ruse she knew was in progress was no small consideration.

"Yup. Speaking of Her Haughtiness, you ought to schedule a little one-on-one time with her yourself."

"My therapy sessions are none of your business."

"I mean training her to be you. Or did you think you're so simple and straightforward that she could mimic you without any practice?"

━━

Charlotte lounged with her feet in the water, dangling off the end of a gilded raft. High salt content made it so that her calves were more buoyant, keeping her toes poking above the surface like little archipelagos. Eric's did likewise. While she wore a two-piece swimsuit and a wide-brimmed hat to shade her eyes from the sun, Eric sported a sky-blue silk bathrobe that covered him nearly to his knees. Wisely or not, he stared straight up into that blinding sunshine.

All around them, little crystals bobbed and drifted with the currents.

Each of the little domes was the top of a buoy. Each buoy was an enclosed city with its own ecosystem and gravity and spectacular view of the ocean all around it. Presently, the inhabitants also had an awe-inspiring vantage on their gods.

In the little corners of her ears, Charlotte could make out the prayers directed her way. While it had become an annoyance, she'd insisted that Eric not remove the ability of the Villagers of Eternity to contact them. The Ritual of Prayer made the process enough of an inconvenience that the villagers didn't overuse the privilege, and neither of them acted on the majority of the suits. But it seemed cruel not to at least allow some provision for redress of grievances.

Presently, one caught Charlotte's ear.

All-Mother Charlotte, my baby is sick. I don't know where else to turn.

"Eric, darling, why are we allowing sick babies in our Utopian worlds?"

The ruler of Eternity growled in the back of his throat. "She's not sick. She's teething. I'm already sending a dream vision to the local midwife to help out. I'm really starting to think we erred too far on the 'let everyone do what they want' side and not enough on the 'here's the basics of how humans work' education."

"Or you could have humans be born knowing all they truly need to know."

"That doesn't sound like being human at all, does it?"

Charlotte sighed, disturbing a formation of clouds. "I suppose not."

"You seem preoccupied. I mean, not just right now, but over the past lifetime and a half or so."

"It's not like out there. The memories of this place dull and mute so easily. I remember the past day in reality like it was yesterday." Eric snickered but didn't interrupt. "I just want you to know that I'm proud of you."

"I know that. You remind me often enough."

"I want you to know that I mean it. I'm not just fluffing your matted-down ego." She didn't mean to imply an "anymore" in there, but Charlotte suspected that they both heard it. "And what we're about to undertake is incredibly dangerous."

"You'll be fine," Eric assured her hurriedly. "You'll be safe here. You'll have backup and—"

"I'm not worried about me. I'm really not. You have by far the harder acting job and by far the more danger if you fail."

"Jessie can't be the easiest person to be," he protested.

So sweet of him, but so, so inaccurate. "I've a growing affection for your sister, but she's the least complex creature you can imagine. She shoots from the verbal hip, but with a few Morphean cheats, I can recollect her reactions to similar circumstances, and with my experience on stage, I can reenact them proficiently. You're impersonating a legendary debater with a vocabulary that dictionaries envy and a literary background to rival the Great Library of Alexandria. Not to mention that he's a glib, cocksure bastard to a degree that I would have found impossible in humans had I not made your father's acquaintance."

"I'll muddle through," Eric assured her.

Charlotte reached across the gap between their lounge chairs and took him by the hand. "I know you will. And you'll allow Jessica and Mort to get your father back safe and sound."

The sky darkened. "And if they don't, I *will* avenge them!" Eric declared with a mischievous grin that said he might be serious but not entirely.

Suddenly, a cacophony assailed Charlotte's ears. Tiny voices pleaded and swore oaths in her direction.

Vengeance for Eric!

In our savior's name, I will avenge you!

Eric, have mercy on us. I beg of you.

All-Mother Charlotte, shield us from All-Father Eric's wrath!

Charlotte shot the nearest floating city crystal buoy a cross look.

"Eriiiiic? Did you forget to make those little cities soundproof?"

———

There was an element of frivolous amusement in subjecting some of Earth's finest chefs to the whims of an unsophisticated palate. After coasting on the coattails of the previous Khosrau's menu atrocities, Hadrian had steered this version into more familiar, comforting, bourgeois selections.

Of late, dating to his recent humoring of a prisoner, the palace kitchens and every visiting gourmet had been falling all over themselves to come up with the perfect imperial hamburger.

The East Wing dining hall was awash in the scent of Kobe beef and Sriracha aioli and a dozen other, subtler smells he couldn't have identified without the help of an azrin's nose.

"Feast! Enjoy! Where you're ending up next, there's scientific chow and the pretentious, meatless offerings of a geriatric tesud." Emperor Khosrau took his seat so that his guests would feel at ease to follow suit. "Just be glad you weren't here for lunch. Those poor bastards assigned to the Martian end of this endeavor would switch places with you before I finished offering the chance."

Polite, even reverent, chuckles came Khosrau's way from all corners of the room.

To call his team handpicked would be giving his own hands too much credit. Of the four he'd be sending along to do the job, he'd met exactly zero of them prior to this formal dinner engagement. But he'd been briefed in full by Vincente.

Commander Elgin Towers would be the team lead. A key operative of Earth Navy Intelligence, his people were the ones providing most of the ground-level intel for the mission in the first place. He knew and trusted the analysts and field agents involved because he'd either trained or served with every last one of them. As a liaison, he was ideally suited to the job.

Lt. Commander Maisie Kearney had an impressive list of scientific credentials. She was, above all, an expert in interrogation, getting a rare chance to apply her skills in the wild, where impediments to restraining, drugging, and torturing her subjects might be minimal. Exquisite observational skills and interpersonal instincts would serve her well.

From the Convocation, two wizards had been put forward as part of the entourage. Even with Mordecai's absence, the *Arete* boasted two middling wizards on staff, plus that absolute madman of a chronomancer, who, Captain Ramsey had assured Khosrau's people, would be kept as far from any involvement with the mission as possible.

Still, it never hurt to have contingencies.

Cornelius Hapsburg was a fleet wizard, recalled from the defense of the *ENV Khartoum* while it was in space dock for repairs. Formally from the Order of Morpheus, he was a rare Merlin adept in several disciplines of magic from fire and brimstone to hand-to-hand armed combat to deciphering and reciphering rune glyphs.

The junior wizard of the pair was an up-and-comer of rare talent. Meyang produced next to no wizards, and it was commonly held that both a lack of innate ability and a species-wide disdain for academic pursuits were to blame. Only multiple intercessions from respected members who'd met him even got Yarzzi Mekou a sniff of Stanford admissions, but the azrin's graduation in two years had proved his detractors wrong. He'd developed a specialty in suppressing the magic of others, a useful talent when his own claws were lethal weapons.

"If all goes according to plan, your considerable skills will be relegated to a backup plan," Khosrau informed them. "Each of you is adept, deadly, cunning, and resourceful. Credit our sworn allies with the same respect. Because should they choose to double-cross us, you will not only be the first to know of their treachery, it will be incumbent upon you to thwart it. These are neither foolish nor trivial individuals, no matter how much their manner suggests otherwise. They are in possession of frighteningly powerful technology as well as enough magic to make adversaries think twice.

"You are to gain their confidence, their trust, and access to their senior officers such that there is no opportunity to work against us in secret. Of course, you will *also* be acting as go-betweens for the operation. All communications from the palace to the *Arete* and vice versa will either be facilitated by or conducted by yourselves. Whatever resources, information, or personnel is required, you will arrange.

"Be aware that your dual allegiance will be an open secret. They will know they are being watched. Do all of you understand the role you're being asked to play?"

Four yesses answered immediately.

"Good. If any of you have reservations or wish to recant your acceptance of this assignment, all you have to lose is glory and prestige. I will bear no ill will, inflict no punishment, and disallow any others to impede your careers if you choose to withdraw. I want four operatives fully committed, fully confident, fully convinced of their ability to carry out their orders."

Silence. Not even the kitchen servant carrying a platter of condiments made a peep as he froze mid-step.

"Good. Any questions, then?"

"These hamburgers are all cooked," Yarzzi pointed out. "I generally—"

Vincente stepped forward, like a medieval gargoyle springing to life from a cathedral rooftop. "Already taken care of. I've alerted the chef, and two uncooked patties are being sent up presently."

The feline grin with its razor fangs made Khosrau damn glad he had his magic to defend himself. "Thank you. Perhaps request another six after those. Even burnt, they smell delicious, and I don't expect to eat the bread."

"Any questions about the mission?" Emperor Khosrau clarified. A hungry silence was his only reply. "Well, then, let's all dig in."

———

Elsewhere in the palace, guitar chords rang out from a six-hundred-year-old antique acoustic that was very nearly in tune. Carl lounged in a bathrobe loosely cinched at the waist and, with his bare feet propped on an ottoman twice that age, he felt his way through a song that was not merely stuck in his head but forcing its way out in a process he compared with childbirth—though not in front of Amy ever again.

"Need a drum track," he muttered, but he also knew that if he asked for one, he'd receive some overpriced computer shitbox that kept perfect time and made him sound like a fucking amateur. Jean always knew how to adjust the tempo of a song to Carl's playing.

Instead of dwelling on the lack of a beat, he wrangled the riff from his brain to his callused fingers. Every few bars, he'd palm the strings and start over. While those fingers of his learned the chord progression and the few plucked notes in between, his brain worked out some lyrics.

Song lyrics were poetry. Poetry was 90 percent access to a rhyming dictionary and 10 percent plagiarism. And a true artist was one who knew what nearly forgotten masterpieces were worth pillaging for emotions, imagery, and riffs.

Through the balcony door, Carl spotted his guard wince.

Every once in a while, he played an off-key note just to catch the reaction. It showed the guy was listening and not just tuning him out.

He'd been getting to know his jailers by name. This shift, Alberto was out in the hallway, checking the servants who delivered meals and fresh laundry. Outside, it was Viswanathan, the music critic. Well, Carl just assumed that part, since the guy had been pretty tight about personal details. But even palace guards had to have hobbies.

Now that he considered it, maybe they didn't. Maybe having their personalities bleached clean was part of the selection process.

Time to test that assumption.

Carrying the heirloom instrument by the neck, he headed over and knocked on the glass of the balcony's French doors.

"What?" Viswanathan demanded.

"You can open the door, you know. I'm not even tempted to jump."

"I'm here for your protection, Mr. Ramsey."

Carl tried the handle and was mildly surprised that there wasn't anything stopping him from opening it.

"Shut that!"

"Sure, sure. Just a minute, though," Carl replied, patting the air with his free hand. "But I need to ask you something. I see the indentation on your finger. Off-duty, you wear a wedding ring."

"That wasn't a question."

"Nah, didn't mean that as my question. What I want to know is whether you've ever been cut off from communications with your... wife?" Carl didn't have a great read on the guy, so he was only guessing that he was the wife-marrying sort.

"Look, I've been briefed. No personal contact. If you have a complaint or request, Corporal Mendoza at the main door will help you."

"That bachelor?" Carl scoffed. "He'd never understand. But I get it. You have to maintain distance in your prisoner/torturer relationships. Forget I said anything."

That struck a nerve. "I'm not *torturing* you."

"Oh. No. Of course not!" Carl replied with exaggerated somberness. Then he knit his brow. "It's my wife you're torturing. If she's heard a damn thing, it's palace reassurances she can't trust and won't believe. But I'm betting your people are just hanging her out to dry completely. I'm sitting here getting drunk, eating like a celebrity chef, and waiting to see if Emperor Khosrau needs any help with that harem of his. She's back home tearing her hair out and aging a year for every day she doesn't hear from me. And while I'll still love a hairless old hag, I've been keeping myself going by looking forward to my young, beautiful wife."

"Your wife is sixty years old."

"Sixty years *young*," Carl corrected. "Besides, she's a month older than me. Calling her old would be tantamount to admitting that I am. And rock stars never get old."

"You're not a rock star. You're a historical recreationist musician. And I don't know what you expect me to do. I'm barely authorized to speak to you on necessary matters. This doesn't qualify. I can't put you in touch with your wife."

"Could you sneak her a love song I've been working on?"

"Sneak? Out of the question!"

"Fine. Don't sneak it. Let your superiors check it for... I don't know, fleet battle plans or whatever-the-fuck top secret intel you're worried I might have. I don't care. I'm horny. I miss my wife, and when you go home and sleep with yours tonight, I want you to remember that Amy's out there somewhere sick to death with worry, and all I'm asking for is for someone to forward her a goddamn love song."

When Viswanathan's gaze strayed to the stack of plastisheet paper on the Victorian-era nightstand, Carl knew he had the guy.

"Fine. I'll take whatever garbage you've written to my lieutenant and forward your request that it be passed along to Mrs. Ramsey."

"Great!" Carl replied, wrapping the guard in a brief, one-armed hug. "Lemme just finish writing it."

He practically threw himself back into the armchair he'd been using and took up strumming his main riff again.

It was one thing trying to come up with a song that would double as a coded message, but the wondering whether he'd ever be able to smuggle the message out of his palace prison cell had proved too much of a distraction.

Now, as he muddled his way through some verses that strained even his musical sensibilities, Carl knew he'd at least have a chance of it reaching Amy.

———

Serifos Supply Depot vanished. Pale gray astral space surrounded the *Scylla* as Captain Ramsey placed her ship back into service. After the agreed-upon hour's travel at 4 AU to put some distance between the pirate shipyard and its most recent customer, they dropped back into realspace.

"Hello, old friend," she told the Black Ocean. After a wistful sigh that curdled up from the toes, she addressed her bridge crew. "Get us back on the omni. I want basic nav updates, comm backlog, and major galactic news ASAP."

God, it felt good being back on a moving starship again. That asteroid had been a rocky coffin. Jamie paced the bridge as her officers reported in.

"Nav charts updated. No major changes to report." Good. That meant nobody had blown up any moons and nothing had gone supernova. It was the least surprising news she could have received.

"Eyndar Empire is in civil war. Emperor died under strange circumstances, and the line of succession turned into a shooting gallery."

"What the fuck?" Jamie exclaimed. "How? Last updates had them stable as hell."

The Eyndar Empire had its own definition of "stable," naturally. For humans, centuries of democracy and the ARGO coalition had established a baseline for their section of the Milky Way. For the eyndar, it was more that the current emperor wasn't embroiled in scandal, surrounded by disloyal fleet admirals, or pissing off his next of kin. Apparently, reports of the latter, at least, had been too optimistic.

"Conflicting reports, ma'am. Working on it."

"Good. Work on it. I want a Current Events lesson on the subject over dinner tonight."

But that wasn't the biggest surprise in store for her.

"Captain, comm backlog coming through. You've got a priority one alert from your niece."

Jamie blew a deflating breath. She had studied Jessie from afar and sized her up in person, but she still hadn't been prepared for just how exhaustingly like a younger copy of herself that kid really was until she started sounding alarms the instant the *Scylla* went comms dark for repairs.

"You got a summary for me?" Jamie asked, hoping she didn't have to go through the rigmarole of sifting the string of increasingly desperate comms.

"Uh... no, ma'am. I think you might want to just put in a comm and act like you didn't hear me say a word."

That bad, huh? Fine. Maybe a final few seconds of blissful ignorance would be all she could hang onto. "Go ahead. Contact the *Arete*."

Not ten seconds passed before Jessie Ramsey appeared on screen wearing a sports bra and ponytail and glistening with a sheen of sweat over those brawny muscles. "AUNT JAMIE!"

"Hi, nice to see you're keeping in shape. We just got out of spacedock and I was given to understand that you tried to get in touch. I warned you we'd be comm dark."

"It's Dad."

Jamie winced. "He found out? From one to five stars, how upset is he?"

"He didn't take 'comm dark' or 'secret pirate spacedock' for an answer, stole a ship, and went off looking for you by himself."

Jamie's wince, still in place on her features, deepened. "Fuck. Does that mean we've got to scour the border colonies for him?" It was a pain in the ass, but with her network of contacts, even an experienced smuggler couldn't hide for too long. Plus, if he was looking for her, poking her head into some of her old business wouldn't be a bad way to get found.

"Ohhhhh, don't get me started. The bastard got himself captured by the Eyndar Empire for forty-year-old war crimes."

"Holy!—wait. Oh, shit. Does this have anything to do with the fuckery going on in the empire right now?"

Jessie knit her brow, still glistening with sweat. "Funny how you're fresh out of Secret Pirate Repair Camp and know about that..."

"It was the first thing in the galactic news roundup!" Jamie protested. "So, what's the plan? We need to work out a prisoner swap. Stage a ground operation."

"No. And it's good that I knew which empire's fuckery you meant because it's Earth that swooped in ahead of our rescue effort and kidnapped Dad."

"Is it kidnapping if he was already being held prisoner?" She's studied up on her brother, but the stories she'd dug up seemed implausible in the aggregate. This lent credence to his unparalleled ability to find trouble.

"They were going to execute Dad for murdering a lot more eyndar than he probably actually killed, but he's technically not a lot safer with Emperor Khosrau."

"Fuck. The Eyndar Empire I could help with. I really don't know what we can do if he's on Earth. But I'll do whatever I can."

"Good. I have a plan, and you and that ship of yours make part of it a lot easier. I need a ride for me and Mort that'll put us on an anonymous transport chain to Earth."

"Mort who?"

"Mort, Mort. The one who—you know what, let's set a rendezvous. I'm short on timetable before the *Arete* gets unwelcome and nosy houseguests, and this shit is going to take some explaining."

"Understood."

Jessie slumped. "No, it's really not, and I'm not sure it'll be understood when I'm finished explaining it. See you soon."

"Copy that." The comm ended abruptly. Mind whirring, Jamie only had one course of action spring to mind. She addressed her bridge crew. "Get us to the *Arete*. Maximum astral."

Charlotte studied herself in the mirror. Another face looked back at her appraisingly. It had been a matter of some embarrassment examining Jessica's body in sufficient detail to pull off the impersonation, more so because she couldn't enact it herself. After two tries at Eric performing the transmogrification, and the resulting semi-androgynous versions of his sister, Charlotte had been forced to allow Mordecai to work the magic, reshaping her to the perfect clone in her mind's eye.

Perfect, she presumed. There would be no tweaking. Her flesh was fired pottery with no hope of turning back to the original clay on her own or making even the most minor of adjustments. With Eric, she'd been confident that a return to her own natural appearance would be a simple matter. But with Mordecai's conjuring, if the worst were to happen, she might be stuck under this enchantment the rest of her life.

Not that it was a bad body. Lithe but muscular. Shorter than her customary though not by much. Femininity was more a stylistic choice than standard issue, and while Charlotte had partaken of cosmetics most of her life, she'd been using tech-free for so long that Aubrey had to be summoned to help use the captain's supply of techno-toiletries.

Now, with lip tint that didn't resemble a clown's makeup and eyeshadow that no longer proclaimed her a bank robber, it was the details she could focus on.

Jessica's uniform fit differently. Aubrey had also commented on the difference as Charlotte struggled to shrug it into a more comfortable arrangement. A more severe, more masculine styling. A bra that was, if she were to judge, a size too tight. Clomping boots of unisex design lent her less height than proper heels but more than regular shoes.

All that was mannequin dressing.

It was the facial expression Charlotte needed to master. Her own studious, serene indifference masked whatever emotions played behind her eyes. It was a practiced expression, fit for her mother's style of command and so ingrained that she slipped into it the moment her attention lapsed.

Jessica's face masked intention with anger and showed more through the cracks than it ought. But so long as Charlotte maintained the *right* diorama behind the cracks of that wall, no one would be the wiser.

There were tricks to theatrical improvisation she could call upon. Ideally, one of these would be the ability to ignore the rampant misplacement of seams in the captain's uniform.

Huffing, Charlotte tugged the hem of her jacket and set her jaw. There. She was done fussing. Jessica didn't fuss. Unless there was a shard of metal weighing at least a kilogram impaled in her flesh, she'd simply choose to overlook physical discomfort.

Years of perfectly tailored clothing and costumers that were the envy of the Poet Fleet, ill-fitting clothing had simply not been among the concerns of her life. And it wasn't that Jessica's uniform fit poorly. It was the body inside that was unfamiliar. She balanced differently; her eye line was slightly wrong. Too many minor details required her attention at slightly more conscious levels of thought than she'd have preferred.

There came a knock at the door.

Charlotte steeled herself and ignored it.

Wizards knocked. Attentive servants knocked for wizards. Presently, Charlotte was neither.

The door chimed. More like it. "What?" she snapped, and

in her head, it didn't sound like Jessica's voice any more so than her own sounded like reproductions. But everyone assured her it was correct.

When the door to the captain's quarters slid open, Mindy awaited her. "Soz. Just had to check. Habits is bad habits, am I right?"

Her security lieutenant fell into step beside her as Charlotte marched out into the halls. Heavy tread. Heel hitting distinctly first. No noticeable hip sway. "No more testing."

"Right oh."

"That means no wink-and-a-nod jokes, no deference to me as a wizard, no helpful suggestions of what the captain might do. Until further notice, I *am* Captain Jessica Ramsey."

"I gots it. I gots it. And you and him ain't gonna be around."

"We have never rendezvoused with the *Scylla*," she reminded the lieutenant as the lift doors closed behind them. "Hangar." The indicators demonstrated that they were in motion despite the lack of physical sensation. "No screwups. We have a grace period while our version of Mort remains aboard, but once he departs, we are at the mercy of the ruse for protection."

The lift doors opened onto the hangar, and Charlotte drew pretense around her like a cloak. She strode forward brusquely —one of her reminder words for the performance. Any stage character, if one became lost or undirected, could fall back on three watchwords for an appropriate behavior.

Charlotte's watchwords for this performance as Jessica Ramsey were: brusque, flippant, confident. She'd have added "impatient" if there were a fourth, but three was the rule as she'd learned it.

Lisa and Daphne waited at the back of an Earth Navy shuttle in anticipation of her arrival. A fresh coat of tint on the vessel still emitted a chemical stink. It displayed no designation, had broadcast no ID when scanners picked it up, and likely had been stripped of any computer records that might allow it to be traced back to Earth.

It could just as easily have been a Mars Navy vessel or a refit by pirates.

But it was their liaisons.

"Give them the go-ahead to disembark," Charlotte ordered.

Lisa nodded and spoke into her TeleJack. Charlotte had opted not to wear Jessica's device. Since adopting a more magical approach to combat, she'd been using it less and less of late. Also, the real Jessica Ramsey had brought it along for her mission.

The four women waited as the shuttle's ramp folded down with a hiss of equalizing pressure. Four emissaries of Earth Empire descended once it touched down. All wore nondescript, casual black clothing devoid of rank insignia, affiliation, or fashion sense.

"Captain Ramsey?" the leader inquired. He approached with a handshake offered, and Charlotte took it. "I'm Elgin Towers, Earth Navy Intelligence. I'll be leading the coordination efforts. Let me introduce my team. My second in command here is Maisiela Kearney—"

"Maisie is fine," the woman added, taking the moment to shake Charlotte's hand as well. It took a reminder of Confidence that Jessica would try to all but break bones in any hand she shook. The woman's faint wince proved that her adjunct display of dominance had worked.

"My two Convocation attachés are Wizard Cornelius Hapsburg, Order of Morpheus, and Wizard Yarzzi Mekou with the Inquisition." The two wizards bowed their heads without taking their hands out of their sleeves. The former of the pair had a typical Convocation look. Slicked-back hair and a trimmed beard. At least fifty years of age unless he tinkered with his appearance. But the other caused Charlotte's breath to catch in her throat.

Azrin.

Charlotte had met her share, of course. Just never as a member of the Convocation. And she knew well enough that this one was checking her scent by the telltale twitch of the nostrils. He was scrawny, taller than Daphne but clearly weaker physically. She'd always found orange fur a rather playful look, common among less serious azrin, and perhaps this one fit that bill in the traditional sense that he was likely a poor candidate to ever lead a pack hunt or claim glory in personal combat.

But his smile was razor sharp.

"I smell their identities. They are who they appear to be," Wizard Yarzzi reported, not taking his eyes off Charlotte's.

The lift doors opened again, and all eyes turned to the one who entered. Mordecai's handiwork had been good enough to fool even an azrin nose. But when the false Mordecai The Brown approached, slouching, hands in his sweatshirt front pocket, a perpetual sneer fixed onto his face, it was Eric's spellcraft that would be put to the test.

"About time you folks showed up," Mordecai The Eric proclaimed grumpily. "Starting to wonder whether I was going to have to walk."

━━━

A whole colony of ants had moved into Eric's guts. It was one thing faking in front of the crew. Even if he messed up completely, he'd just get laughed at or scolded, and his ego had grown leathery to both. But now, with these strangers from Earth aboard the *Arete*, he was the lynchpin of the whole operation, and Eric didn't even know what a lynchpin was.

When Elgin Towers introduced himself, Eric merely glanced down at the proffered hand until it was withdrawn.

"So... Wizard Mordecai... we have arranged a series of transports to get you to Mars under an assumed identity," the Earth Navy spy told him. "Lieutenants Mercedes and Calloway will be piloting you on the first leg of the journey."

From inside the shuttle, up front where the pilot and copilot sat, a pair of ununiformed officers waved.

Mort... Mort... Mort... Eric reminded himself. The old wizard had a dizzying intellect but a puerile sense of humor, dark and blunt. "They've been warned that if I'm double-crossed, they're the first to go, right?"

Towers smiled. "There won't be any double crosses."

But Eric wasn't done because he couldn't imagine Mort allowing anyone else the last word on this issue. "Glad to hear it. But on the off chance that one of my innumerable transports were to run into an expected catastrophe, and I somehow manage to survive—which is more likely than you're probably willing to grant—I'll be turning you into a porcelain commode and donating you to a stuunji curry restaurant."

The blink in the hardened intelligence operative's eyes told Eric that he'd struck the right note with his threat. Proper, Mort-ish threats were something he'd gone over with the real Mort a lot before Aunt Jamie stopped by to pick up him and Jessie. A good threat had to be wildly magical, imaginative, over-the-top spiteful, and evocative of a level of horror that would give pause to anyone on the receiving end.

Most importantly, any threat had to sound utterly casual. No one was going to believe that a wizard was going to perform elaborate rituals or devote decades to a massive revenge scheme. Plenty of dark wizards, of course, *would* go to such ridiculous lengths, but no one believed them until they were dangling over the yawning chasm of a newly erupting volcano or the ninth generation of horse-sized vampire bats had finally proved up to the task of hunting down the prey they were bred to chase.

Threats that sounded offhanded, that sounded so easy yet so cruel, those were the sweet spot, as Mort had explained it.

Towers gulped. "Of course. No funny business."

Eric waggled a finger in the man's face, pointedly ignoring his wizard bodyguards as inconsequential. "Just remember that, even if he wants me dead at the end of all this, Emperor Schnoz-Grow is counting on me to retake Mars for him."

"Everyone involved is either well aware of that fact or entirely ignorant of your identity and role in this matter," the spy assured him.

Eric gave a curt nod before turning to Charlotte, presently disguised as Jessie. "You just keep that brother of yours out of this business. He's not suited to it. And well intentioned or not, he'll bollocks up the works if you let him."

"I've assigned Commander Webber full-time to keeping him away from the operation," Charlotte replied, mostly sounding like Jessie and probably good enough that no one who hadn't grown up with her would have known any better.

Eric gave his Mortest harrumph. "Well, no point dawdling. I didn't bring luggage. Ready when the chauffeurs are."

On his way to the ramp, he caught the azrin wizard testing the air with his nose. First off, Eric dearly wanted to know all about the azrin who'd joined the Convocation and how that had all come to pass. But more Mortishly, he had to be offended.

"Rude to sniff people. If you've ever wanted to find out what charred azrin fur smells like, I can provide that scent for the rest of your life."

The azrin took a step back and shrank inside his robes. "No offense, Mighty One."

Eric smirked. Mort would have appreciated that. He then marched up the ramp, bursting into song. "Off we go, into the wild black yonder..."

As it turned out, neither he nor Mort could sing worth a damn, so he didn't even need to be on key.

———

Leading the morning briefings would be a nagging chore, but one suited to Charlotte's talents. Those same briefings, however, would now include four avowed spies, none friendly to her cause, and she'd be performing a stage act simultaneously.

Arrayed throughout the Briefing Room, the conspirators of what was now being called Operation Ares' Hammer gathered their datapads and their coffee mugs. The meeting had gone well. Earth's plan seemed both plausible and well considered. From the *Arete*, Charlotte and her crew would be monitoring the feed from operatives already on Mars and providing Eric with assurances that Mort would want to maintain his motivation and trust.

The *Arete* was being held hostage.

Surely, the quartet from Earth had to know that the hidden wizard kept out of sight and in reserve was their secret defense. With Mort supposedly en route to Mars, neither Charlotte nor Sparta could be expected to adequately fend off two formidable emissaries from the Convocation.

Charlotte actually knew of Wizard Cornelius by reputation, if not personally. Deployed with Earth Navy, he had a future among the leadership of the Order of Morpheus after his tour of duty. She had to do a mental reset when the wizard lingered after the meeting to walk her out.

"Captain Ramsey, if you don't mind a word in private?"

Lisa, who'd been lurking outside the Briefing Room waiting to pick up her assigned escortee, nodded an approval.

"Sure. What's up?" Charlotte replied, barely slowing on her way past.

The Morphean wizard fell into step at her side. "I have my own personal reservations about whether the Mordecai The Brown we dispatched to Mars is in fact the genuine article. My views are not unique in this matter."

Charlotte shrugged. "Little late to be second-guessing, isn't it?"

"Not at all. Now that you're free of his direct influence, I'd like permission to examine you and your top officers for signs of—"

Charlotte stopped in her tracks, one of Jessie's more annoying habits in roving conversations. "Stopping you right there. Mort warned us you might try this. He set up barricades or some shit in our minds. If you think he's a fraud, by all means, try to go digging around behind my eyes. Your three companions will be informed of your actions, and your next of kin will be presented your remains in a little plastic takeaway bag."

"You're placing a lot of faith in the words of an avowed traitor, murderer, and fugitive."

"You're placing a lot of suffering on the line if you're wrong. The Emperor vouches for—"

"Emperor Khosrau is young and foolish, even if he's powerful enough to turn his mistakes to ash. He is at far greater risk from deception than from open confrontation, and this seems like the perfect opportunity to overexpose his plots."

This was far more open an admission than Charlotte would have expected from such a high-profile Morphean. Did he really respect Jessica so little that he'd speak this bluntly in front of her? She had to realize on the captain's behalf and respond appropriately—or, more in character, *inappropriately.*

"Thank you for your concern, but go fuck yourself. Either the guy is legit, and he's out to save my dad because the two have been friends for decades. Or... he's a mastermind who's planning to stir up protests on Mars, infiltrate a security lockdown, and exterminate 94 members of the Martian Military Government *as a ploy.* Just to fuck with you people."

While she was by no means a wilting flower, it took conscious effort to roll her vocabulary through the mud to make herself sound more like Jessica.

"I take your point, but Mordecai The Brown has been confirmed dead by reliable sources."

Charlotte made her way to the lifts with Wizard Cornelius in tow. Right as the doors opened, she turned and blocked his path, staring him down from half a head shorter, even in her combat boots. "Look, believe what you want. But I believe he's really Mort because Mort's the only bastard in the galaxy that cares enough about my dad for this bullshit the emperor pulled to work on him. *Intelligas,* asshole?"

She took a step and backed into the lift, not leaving a path for the wizard to follow without pushing past her. Just as the doors closed, Charlotte made eye contact with Lisa, coming up from the hall behind them to take over chaperone duty.

Once she was alone in the lift, Charlotte allowed Jessica's replica body to slump against the wall and seethe out a sigh of mixed frustration and released stress. Operation Ares' Hammer couldn't end soon enough for her liking.

———

Daphne didn't like being assigned to the Senior Liaison for Operation Ares' Hammer, but after a week solid of shadowing

Commander Elgin Towers, the pair had come to an understanding...

The feeling was mutual.

Towers was a slimy weasel with persistently shifty eyes and not enough skin to stretch over his muscles. His breath reeked of a health concoction of vegetables and base proteins, and his antiperspirant contained an illegal pheromone that Daphne had reported on before the end of her first day babysitting the spook. Those not under the protection of H-tech immune systems had been given a counteragent by Dr. Richelieu to negate any reason-addling effects of the chemicals.

The Earthling must have been flustered when his off-hours attempts to pump *Arete* crew members for information were met with cold indifference rather than hot-blooded eagerness.

Now, Daphne watched from a pace away as Trebla established the secure connection to Boston Prime that would be the only line of communication between the Haathee Federation embassy vessel and the birthplace of humanity.

An Earth Navy admiral who didn't identify himself appeared on screen. The background was pure black. Not dark for lack of lighting, just tinted a shade that ate nearby color, cast no reflection, and left the front-lit speaker on the far end of the comm as a ghost floating in nothingness.

"Report."

"Sir, operations are proceeding on schedule. The instigator has completed insertion. Local teams have reported full cooperation despite an unhelpful attitude. The cover identity is being seasoned with the subject as we speak."

"Impediments on your end?"

Daphne watched for it, but the master spy's eyes didn't even twitch in her direction. "Relations have been goal oriented. So long as our interests remain aligned, I don't foresee any troubles on that front."

This didn't sound like a conversation that was liable to drag, and she didn't dare miss her chance. Daphne spoke up. "I'd like an updated proof of life. The captain was quite keen."

"Denied," the admiral replied. "The only one we're concerned about is the instigator. Unless he's asking, the answer will continue to be 'no.' And I know you're not in contact with him."

"Captain R—"

"The captain," Towers interjected.

Stupid, paranoid, bullshit protocols. If they believed for an instant that the comm might be compromised, none of them should have spoken a word. And if they thought that any enemies couldn't readily puzzle out that "the instigator" was Mort or that "the captain" was Jessie Ramsey, they were fools.

Still, she'd get nowhere if they cut her out of their little game.

"The captain is quite insistent. She'll at least need some reassurance."

"The insurance policy is the most dangerous prisoner we've held in living memory. The emperor's words, not mine. But I'll follow my orders and treat him as such. Follow yours and don't ask again."

"I'll speak with the captain," Towers promised on her behalf, bristling the fur at the back of Daphne's neck.

The comm ended.

"You know this will end badly if Carl Ramsey is harmed," Daphne warned.

Elgin Towers gave her such a smirk. "That's not my end of the operation. But I fail to see how it would be in the emperor's best interest to renege on the deal."

"A failure of imagination on both your part and his," Daphne countered. "And I'll be watching that you keep your end going smoothly."

"It's all just one big game of Spin-the-Blaster. I'm sure you could tear my throat out. Cornelius or Yarzzi will kill you. Then we find out whether that kid brother of Ramsey's that you've been hiding from us can avenge you. Meanwhile, Kearney's jacking your comms to relay the kill order to Earth.

"No one wins unless we *all* play nice."

Daphne forced her hands to relax.

Her claws slowly slid back into their sheaths.

"Another failure of imagination," Daphne told him as the pair headed off to the dining lounge for dinner.

Timing wasn't everything, but it was important enough that Jessie's final departure for Earth felt long overdue by the time she stepped onto the starliner. The delays along the way had been manufactured, not real, and were designed to give Eric and his merry band of Earth operatives time to foment chaos on Mars. Two days from now, she and Mort would exit this transport and breathe natural air for the first time since the so-called Earth-like eyndar homeworld.

Mort flashed the Convocation sigil in the ticket taker's face. When he snapped, "She's with me," to cover Jessie's lack of ticket in addition to his own, it was with Aunt Tiffany's voice.

After all, he was borrowing everything else about her.

The fact that Mort knew Aunt Tiffany well enough to make such a convincing disguise bothered her. Sure, the two of them had worked together enough when Mort was Emperor Khosrau, but the level of detail was uncanny. And unlike her brother, Mort was well familiar with human anatomy and lacked any shyness about it. Their shopping had acquired him a wardrobe that matched Aunt Tiffany's aesthetic. Leggings, knee-length skirt, high-top sneakers, a sleeveless blouse with a baggy-sleeved cable-knit cardigan over it in a dull shade of beige. Crystal spectacles rounded out the ensemble.

And yet, Mort couldn't get the ponytail to sit right without Jessie's help.

Her own disguise was less specific. As a young woman of indeterminate age, she was Aunt Tiffany's height, underfed, with dark, darting eyes and jaw-length black hair prone to tangles. Her cover was a colonial orphan that Wizard Tiffany had tagged as a potential apprentice. While she had a whole cover ID put together, they were keeping her as much a mystery as possible so that no one could dig into her vacant background story before they arrived on Earth.

"Right this way, ladies," a steward bid them. He hustled ahead of them, passing rows of seated passengers on bargain fares before arriving at a stateroom and activating the door. "If you have any troubles, the panel just inside the door will summon an attendant. Liftoff is in just over 30 minutes. Dinner service will be along in about an hour. Would you like to order in advance?"

Mort wandered inside, giving their accommodations a once-over. It was a fairly bland sleeper cabin. Two couches faced one another and could pull out to become a pair of beds with room for a leg or arm to hang into the gap between. They had a lone window and no private washroom.

"Can I order a better room?" Mort asked idly, staring out the window at a pollen-smeared view of the Denton Colony Starport in what seemed like a local springtime bloom.

"These *are* the best accommodations we had available."

"What about the ones that weren't?" Mort inquired.

Jessie saw the gulp before the steward answered. "We do have family sleepers and first-class suites, but—"

"That'll do. One of those."

"But, mistress!" Jessie objected.

Mort shook his head, sending Aunt Tiffany's ponytail swaying. "No, no. You're done living in squalor. I told you wizards get to live the good life, and I'm not making a liar of myself in your first week as my apprentice. Boy, clear the nicest suite you've got. Pay the occupants what you need to. Send the bill to Boston Prime, and leave yourself a generous tip while you're at it."

"But the people in those suites are—"

"Less important than me, I can fucking assure you," Mort replied, and in that instant, Jessie could have sworn he was Aunt Tiffany.

After training in Mortania for what felt like a million years, Jessie had eventually learned to pick up on subtle uses of magic around her. Eric was like a bubbling teapot that someone left on the burner and occasionally poured more water into. Charlotte was a mirror-smooth pond with rare ripples of activity. Sparta was a distant brook, always burbling just out of view.

Given his reputation and history, Jessie would have expected that Mort would be like traveling with an ocean, all crashing waves and the occasional tsunami. Instead, Mort was nothing at all. Even blatantly working magic in front of her, Jessie couldn't tell he was doing anything at all supernatural.

Right now, watching the reaction of the terrified steward, she suspected that, in this case, the only magic in play was self-confidence. Plenty of entitled busybodies demanded shit like it belonged to them. Few could convincingly convey that horrific consequences would befall anyone who stepped out of line the way Mort could.

He hadn't raised his voice. He hadn't flashed lightning or fire from those deceptively thin fingertips with their pink nail tint. He hadn't even closed the distance to put himself in the steward's personal space.

But an hour later, the pair were watching sickly gray astral space out a much larger window as they dined on mediocre steak and soggy green beans that represented the pinnacle of starliner cuisine.

"You didn't have to be such an asshole about getting this suite," Jessie scolded once the waiter had departed after leaving their thawed frozen cheesecake desserts. The more she talked in private, the more she'd get used to the ridiculous new voice this body came with.

"Oh, but I did," the disguised wizard assured her. "Tiffany Bell is a notorious bitch when she travels. Even as emperor, I'd get complaints. In fact, anyone who reported her traveling public starliners or staying in anything below a five-star hotel and *not* filing complaints would raise suspicions."

Jessie snickered. "So, it takes five-star service to please her?"

"No. I rather suspect those stodgy old institutions just have a policy against complaining about Convocation guests. Frankly, I think that's largely the difference in *getting* that fifth star."

Glancing around after popping a bite of bland, freezer-burned cheesecake into her mouth, Jessie tried to make sense of the runes Mort had sketched. "Are we... I dunno, totally free to talk?"

"Totally," Mort confirmed, reverting to character. "Ask whatever the fuck you want. Like it matters."

"Right, mistress," Jessie replied teasingly. "I was just wondering—"

"We are *not* doing the mistress/apprentice thing. I'm your teacher. Call me either Wizard Tiffany or Librarian."

"Do people actually call her that? Or librarians in general?"

"No. But you're new and it reminds people I could stuff their own arm down their throat far enough that they could wipe their ass from the inside."

Jessie cringed involuntarily. "Ugh."

"That. Right there. That reaction is what comes from a good threat. Now, go ahead. You had a question."

"What's the plan when we get to Earth? Just... show up at the palace? Demand to see the emperor?"

"Close. But not quite. I'll have a stop to make first. I may have given up the puppet with the nominal power in the empire, but I've still got friends on Earth."

"Friends? You?"

"Fine. More like admirers."

Jessie raised an eyebrow.

Rather than harrumph, Mort wrinkled Aunt Tiffany's nose. "Would you believe power-hungry kindred spirits with a penchant for mayhem?"

"Just what the hell are you dragging me into?"

"Um... getting Jessica and Eric their father back, dumbass. But we're going to want a distraction, and I've got a plan you're going to hate, so I'm not fucking telling you. Deal with it."

For the first time since he'd taken on this persona, Jessie was questioning whether she'd rather have the real Aunt Tiffany along.

———

A knock at the door startled Tiffany awake. In Tiffsylvania, the sound had been reimagined as a fire alarm in the food court, where she'd been enjoying a raspberry gelato with Lacey Cowette, one of her favorite actresses whom she'd never met in real life.

Whoever was at the door, it had better be good.

Upon rolling over, Tiffany discovered a berm of flesh. Right. Raul. A smile snuck onto her lips.

Raul had been almost like a boyfriend for the duration of

this enforced vacation. Except he did whatever he was told, treated her with the utmost respect and deference, and—most crucially—she *had* a Raul. Boyfriends had never really stuck around, and she'd never been clingy enough to try convincing one.

Two quick slaps on the rump and a shove to get him to take a hint, and Raul groggily rolled onto his back for her to start the morning off right. But before Tiffany could make her move, the knock on the door repeated.

"Shit," she whispered. The *Neptune's Reverie* crew hadn't bothered her all trip. She hadn't pre-ordered breakfast from room service, nor had she requested a fucking wake-up call.

On her way to the door, she scooped a silk bathrobe off the floor and cinched it, satisfying the bare minimum clothing to avoid a scandal. Not that she cared about scandal, per se, but scandalized technologists ended up causing delays, and delays were bullshit.

"What?" she demanded when the door was only halfway open, expecting some concierge or uninvited visitor. Then, a blink later, she realized it was the captain of the *Neptune's Reverie*, in full dress uniform. "Oh. Morning. Fancy seeing you here."

High-ranking nobodies were never a good sign. Tiffany was keenly aware that people didn't like dealing with her. She did her best to make sure of that. When anyone with the authority to have someone *else* interact with her chose to do so themselves, that was a tip-off that bad news was headed her way.

Or really good news. The couple times *that* had ever happened, someone had tried to make hay from her goodwill. But Convocation librarians in general weren't magnets for good news. Collections librarians from the Vault of the Plundered Tomes even less so.

"Wizard Tiffany," the captain told her with a curt, military nod. "The *Neptune's Reverie* will be cutting its journey short, I'm afraid. We'll be at the wharf in Pickert's Landing by breakfast."

"How long is that?"

The captain pulled out an antique-looking pocketwatch with a modern chrono set into the face. "Thirty-seven minutes."

"We having a science problem that you're here to apologize for, or is this a specifically *me* issue?"

"His Majesty, Emperor Khosrau Blackstone, First of His Name, has issued orders recalling you to Earth. There will be transportation awaiting you as soon as we arrive at port."

"Fuck."

"No time for that, I'm afraid," the captain deadpanned, and it took Tiffany a split second to realize the joke as the man cast a glance past her.

Raul had fallen back to sleep. He'd been a good sport all trip, but his career had made him into something of a night owl. Since she could wake up refreshed after three or four hours of sleep, Tiffany had been wearing the guy out. "Any chance I can keep him?" she asked, hooking a thumb at her sleeping companion.

"I'm afraid I cannot speak for Mr. Kensington."

Tiffany scrunched her face. She didn't want to know his real name. That made him too persony. Raul was an amenity for the trip, like the hot tub or the chocolate fountain. "Mr. Kensington" sounded like someone who paid taxes and called his mom "Mother." At least she didn't have a first name to go with it. Finding out he was a "Bob" or a "Clark" would have crushed her little vacation dream man back into reality.

Perhaps sensing her disappointment, the captain made an attempt to placate her. "I can have the kitchen prepare you anything you like prior to your disembarkation. If you'd like a moment to freshen up and gather your—"

Tiffany snapped her fingers.

A whirlwind of clothes had the captain shielding his face with his arms and taking a step back from the door.

Seconds later, a fully dressed Tiffany Bell adjusted her glasses and hoisted her duffel bag over her shoulder.

"Can I get that for you?" the captain offered.

"Too heavy. I've got it." Instead of passing him the duffel, she handed over the silk bathrobe. Raul was stirring, the maelstrom having roused him from his well-earned slumber. "Room's all yours. Enjoy. Charge anything you like to the emperor."

Under her breath, as she followed the captain to the dining room, Tiffany added, "Because that fucker owes me."

―――

Eric perched on a park bench with a half-empty bag of Jake's Authentic Breadcrumbs amid a flock of well-sated seagulls who, nonetheless, wanted the other half. Of course, no one *saw* Eric doing this. Certainly none of the residents of New Vancouver, the seat of the Martian Military Dictatorship. No, what they saw was Eric pretending to be Mordecai The Brown pretending to be Hadrian the Brown pretending to be Mordecai The Brown pretending to be Quford Tannenbaum, local. His quirk was correcting people who saw it spelled and tried to pronounce it *kweh-ferd* rather than rhyming it with Buford like a good Martian name should.

Of course, that's not what Eric's handlers believed. Well, they didn't care about the name. Eric was just pretending differently with them. To them, he was Hadrian the Brown pretending to be Quford Tannenbaum. The emperor, of course, was Hadrian The Brown pretending to be Khosrau Blackstone, and he was of the opinion that Eric was Mordecai The Brown pretending to be him pretending to be Quford Tannenbaum.

Mort and Jessie, off on the more interesting and dangerous half of the mission, knew the rest but probably wouldn't have guessed about the Quford alias specifically.

But someone knew about Quford. Someone knew he was here. Someone was well aware that he'd be feeding the birds in violation of a piddling local ordinance, a sure sign that Martian waterfowl lacked voting rights, because *they* certainly seemed to be in favor of his activities.

Less so the local constabulary.

"Sir, no feeding the wildlife."

Eric glanced in the direction of the dry, gruff, authoritarian dictate. Mild though it was, it came prepackaged with the implicit threat of a drubbing if he mouthed off or refused the order. But there would be no escalation today.

"Surry, sur," Eric replied. "My mustake." It had taken days getting this accent right. New Vancouver had its quirks, but nothing on par with the famous New Calgary accent. Hollyworld always exaggerated it, and Eric had to unlearn his humorous version to make a native Martian believe his.

Not that it mattered for this particular patrol officer. More for bystanders. When the pair made eye contact, Eric spotted the closed pupils, showing that the man wasn't even seeing him. A more diligent controller might have created the illusion of pupils, since once someone noticed the uninterrupted mirror-like iris, it was hard to ignore—or forget. But Eric was the only other person within bread-chucking distance in any direction.

"No fine today. Just don't let me catch you at it again."

Eric cleared his throat as he rolled the top of his bread bag closed. "Koind of yuh, sur. Moight I buy yuh a cup of cuffee?"

"I wouldn't mind a tall mug about now. Shift's off in twenty. Meet me at Sweet Spoons, but I'm buying. Can't be taking bribes, even if it's just caffeine."

"Understuud, sur. Be there fur sure."

The park didn't have one of those big public chronos, so instead of waiting a measured twenty minutes, he let Squadron 33 1/3's cover of *Baba O'Riley* play in his head four times all the way through. They had a recorded version that he enjoyed and knew by heart, even the parts with no words—which, frankly, was a lot of that one, to the point where he sang along with the doot-doo-deedly-doot-doo parts.

At the approximate time, Eric crossed the park and headed into Sweet Spoon, where he found the patrol officer waiting for him with two paper mugs.

The cafe was quiet. Patrons sat in front of coffees and pastries, not touching either. Not conversing. Not gesturing or checking datapads or even looking bored. It was a walk-in holo-projector on pause.

"See us out back," the officer told him, only moving his mouth and not even glancing in Eric's direction. "Take the coffee."

Having witnessed far weirder sights in his day, even outside the Village of Eternity, Eric took his beverage and gave a test sip as he went behind the counter and into the back room of the cafe.

Not sweet enough. For a place with sweet in the *name*, he found this shabby and took a handful of sweetener packets from the counter on his way through.

When the swinging door shut behind him, the sounds of a bustling cafe picked up as if they'd never stopped.

"Follow me," a woman ordered. She was brown-haired and brown-eyed, with suntanned skin and muted lip tint. The sleeves of her white blouse were rolled to the elbows, the very picture of Not A Wizard. Again, at least if one were to go by Hollyworld stereotypes. Eric was beginning to wonder if this whole conspiracy had been given to Earth Navy covert operatives and Convocation wizards or a casting director and executive producer.

Eric knew the signs of a *real* wizard. Sharp eyes that would take in all their surroundings and *think* about them. A bearing that suggested safety when danger blatantly lurked on all sides. More crucially, he could sense the little bubble of influence with the universe, where the laws of physics awaited permission before proceeding, like a pedestrian signal at a street corner.

Knowing that he was expecting a wizard to meet him, Eric followed.

The Sweet Spoon had been one storefront amid a strip mall beneath an apartment complex and above who-knew-what. Eric didn't have ground-penetrating sight or real divination. Short of creating a new time loop and running ahead to check out where he was being led, the access door and downward staircase unfolded a mystery before him.

A supply room, mostly but not completely cleared of barrels and crates and grime, held two other wizards besides his escort.

"First off, are you or are you not Mordecai The Brown?" one of the newcomers asked. He was slim and shrewd with a gaudy, oversized emerald ring on one finger. He had bushy blond hair and deep-set eyes.

"I am," Eric replied, switching to his gravelly Mort impression. "And you are?"

"I'm Jared. Order of Hephaistos. My companions are Xilena from the Order of Morpheus." Eric's escort nodded to confirm her identity. "And Sambrina with the Order of Athena."

Xilena spoke up. "I was warned not to verify your identity through standard checks. I wanted to hear it from you. What would happen if I looked into your eyes?"

Eric shrugged. "Whatever I wanted."

"I'm quite adept. Most wizards wouldn't even notice."

"A year would pass before you could blink to break the connection," Eric warned. "In that year, I could convince you of anything, pull your consciousness into mine and imprison it, make you experience a reality so convincing that you wouldn't even know that I hadn't let you out, or simply pinch out the light of your soul like a candle flame. And in any scenario, I could make you forget the initial eye contact, so, right now, you can't be certain I haven't already."

Sambrina shuddered. "I warned you not to ask."

"Glad you're on our side," Jared commented.

A smile and a quick round of handshakes, maybe an icebreaker game to get to know one another. Eric suppressed all these natural inclinations and picked from the scripted scenarios the real Mort had armed him with.

"For now. You'd do best to keep up your end if you want to remain on such good terms. I've heard buzzing from your people that I've somehow cheated death. Let me assure you, I cheated no one. That fucker owed me and is paying back a considerable loan. Understood?"

The other three nodded.

"Good. Now, let's plan the slaughter of fourscore and fourteen martial lawbreakers and go our separate ways."

"Yes, Wizard Mordecai," Xilena replied. "If you'll permit me, I have the guest list for the Martian Planetary Party convention, where 86 of our 94 will be in attendance on the climactic third day. We need provisions to either get the others to New Vancouver Civic Arena for day three or round them up concurrently..."

Eric listened as the Morphean wizard droned on. Jared had props he conjured, models of the interior and exterior of the venue. Sambrina reviewed Martian security protocols and magical protection details.

All the while, Eric knew he was just here to stall for time. Everyone was going to be so surprised when day three of that convention arrived and they didn't have an empire to worry about on Earth anymore.

━━

There were ten men in his meeting. Ten loyal, unimpeachable, steadfast defenders of the Martian way of life gathered around. Supreme General Bob Randall glanced up and down the two equal rows of five steely pairs of eyes, making contact with each in turn.

"Gentlemen, good morning. Have a seat." The supreme general led by example, and not until the second his ass touched the chair did a single one of his advisers flinch to park theirs. "Convention is two days out. Speeches are in rewrites. Security is going over the final arrangements. We've got the goddamn *cakes* on ice and ready to go for the welcome shindig. Why am I hearing that we're opening up the platform again?"

"It's the reunification statement," General Portobello answered. "Polling low double-digits."

"Why are we polling at all?" General Bob snapped. "We're not running for office. We're rounding up votes. The opposition party supports me. If by some miracle our patsy wins, he'll step aside and hand back the wheel."

"We still need to govern," Vice Admiral Quatermain reminded him.

"*Thank* you for that brilliant insight." He paused as the door opened and a cart bearing coffee and donuts hovered in, steered by a marine staff sergeant. As if flipping a switch, the supreme general turned deadpan and calm. "Dark roast. Synth milk. No sweetener." Then, just as abruptly, he shifted back to haranguing his underlings. "We are not a bunch of candy-ass consensus-peddlers. We can't keep pretending that every decision can endure ten committee meetings, hearings, two roll call votes, reconciliation, another round of votes, and a 90-day grace period from signing to taking effect. Sure, if you're looking to build a new aqueduct, your timeframe is fine. But if you're at war—and we are—then there's no time to be standing at the urinal holding our dicks. Piss, shake, and zip. Next issue."

"Would you like that on some posters?"

There were chuckles around the room, and even General Bob joined in. He could see it. He could envision the neckless, brainless slobs that kept Mars chugging along to get behind that message. But it would piss off a lot more people, funny though it was, and he needed people obeying orders, not grousing about a goddamn propaganda campaign.

"Make up the posters. They go on the walls in your office," the supreme general ordered to another round of chuckles.

"In all seriousness, Supreme General, we'll have a better response to the convention if we disavow Earth and make a case for a permanent Martian hegemony. The public wants us to beat Earth at their own game, not continue this endless stalemate of a war."

The characterization of the war as a stalemate was a comforting lie, and every man in the room knew it. Mars wasn't going to *lose* the war, but they were taking worse losses than Earth with fewer resources to replace them. Mars Navy had the ships and manpower to continue fighting for the foreseeable future, but the homefront would bear the brunt of the economic impact. Rationing. Drafts. Shortages. Confiscations. Planetized companies. Dark magic. Every option was on the table—the table in question being the supreme general's nightstand in his private residence. None of them would be necessary if there was peace between the capital planets of the two empires.

"No."

"Yes, sir," Portobello replied with a salute. "Just had to make you aware."

"Consider me aware. That's the last I want to hear about peace until after the convention. There's only one peace I want, and it involves Emperor Khosrau's neck in a noose and his feet off the ground. Half the xenos in the galaxy are laughing their asses off at the sight of humans fighting humans. Even split damn near straight down the middle, Mars and Earth are still the two dominant military forces in civilized space. No, the end of this war is Earth's surrender or the death of every last fighting Martian. Understood?"

"YES, SIR!" the officers around the room replied smartly.

"Good. Now, let's get back to planning my 'coronation.'"

"You mean convention?" someone dared ask.

"You heard me..."

⸻

"Keep talking," Harmony instructed her patient. Prone on the examination table, Britney had the back of her skull exposed as Harmony swapped out a Generation One Harmony-Tech Drone Factory for a Generation Two model. Twenty percent larger than the original version, the Generation Two also featured two thin protrusions that would nestle into the tissue of the occipital lobe. The nanopermeable structure would allow for rapid-response drone deployment to the brain.

"About what?"

"Anything you like. It's best practice for neurosurgery to

keep a patient vocal. It's a quicker indicator as to anything going wrong than most scanners can pick up. And without a full team here—"

"I get it. Substandard care because I'm the only one qualified to assist you," Britney joked. Or, at least, Harmony *hoped* she was joking.

The insertion process was the only delicate part of the operation. She'd dialed down her motor control to the absolute finest her muscles could manage. It wasn't even her own neurons controlling her fingers. There was a pre-programmed subroutine running that she was just managing via her datagoggles.

"I can't tell whether it's psychosomatic or real, but I *feel* dumber without the old unit in there."

"I had it completely expel its payload before removal. You shouldn't notice, but if anything, you have increased capacity for the moment."

"I guess. I know the factories aren't doing the computing. But it *feels* like they should be."

"Factories are just schools. The drones themselves are the students and teachers. All the brainpower is in the collective minds of the machines."

"So, what's the upside of this new one?"

It was a fine time to be asking that, immobilized and mid-procedure. When Britney had agreed so readily and been available immediately for the upgrade, Harmony had presumed that her assistant had been keeping abreast of the technical publications she'd been banking for once this could all go public. All of them were available to Britney.

Rather than scold, Harmony summarized.

"Well, the main benefits will be an expected 20 percent increase in drone production and an increase in drone neural response rate that will need extensive measurement to quantify. Theoretical models suggest up to a 60 percent improvement."

"Downsides?" Britney asked with a note of trepidation.

"You'll need to consume roughly one beet's worth of extra nutrients per day. I've already updated your diet in the system."

"Thanks? I guess."

"If you're feeling anxious, I can reduce your neurotransmitter rates in your hippocampus."

"I'd rather you didn't."

"Suit yourself. But sometimes it's best to separate personal feelings from consequential activities."

Activity monitors suggested that if all her motor neurons had been connected, Britney would have sat up at that statement. Luckily for both the patient and the advancement of galactic medical science, the neural block *was* in place, and there wasn't so much as a newton of force applied to the cranial clamps locking Britney's skull motionless for the delicate operation.

"What do you mean consequential?" the patient demanded.

"Activities that contribute to your professional life. Ones that require a degree of emotional separation."

A twinkling in the brain activity monitor where the neck muscles were controlled suggested an attempt to nod. "I get you. Kind of how you didn't knock that Earth spook's block off when he congratulated you on being a traitor to Mars."

"Precisely," Harmony replied offhandedly. Britney didn't need to know that the night after that incident, she'd booked some solo time in the gym and pounded her knuckles red on the martial arts equipment to the point where she'd had to come back with a blood-hazard cleanup kit after treating her injuries in Med Bay.

"Are you... not feeling anything now?"

"It's not an absence of feeling. It's a lack of neurochemical impairment. We can set you up with an easy-to-switch protocol to—"

"I'd rather not."

"I just know that if I weren't using the Harmony-Tech Drones, I'd be losing sleep, eating poorly, and generally irritable and depressed by the current state of Mars."

"How'd you manage before?"

"There are medical solutions. They're just far inferior. Trust me, I've investigated, studied, vetted, overseen trials for, and co-invented numerous treatments. I've never felt better."

"You mean felt less."

"Fewer disruptive episodes. I can feel everything I need to right now, and presently, you're benefiting from improved medical care."

"Will I be eligible for seeing those other feelings later tonight?"

Harmony smirked. The procedure was nearly finished. All she had to do was close up the surgical site and re-enable motor control for the patient. "How about I teach you how to adjust the settings on mine if you let me tinker with yours?"

There was a long pause. Harmony wasn't touching neurons directly anymore, so there was little chance that something had gone wrong medically.

"I... I think maybe tonight you should just spend time with Xrista."

━━━

Clouds raced overhead, viewed through two layers of glassteel, one motionless, the other rocketing past in a blur of structural supports spaced 100 meters apart. Of course, in actuality, those supports were motionless and it was the pod of Jessie and

Mort's transatlantic tram traveling over 6000 kph through a vacuum tube.

Few planets boasted that kind of infrastructure. For nearly any other world, such a grand project would have been for vanity's sake or a technological proof of concept. Here on Earth, it was just the 8:15 Green Line commuter shuttle from Lisbon to Boston.

Mort still looked like Aunt Tiffany. He propped his sneakers on a replica duffel bag identical to Aunt Tiffany's. He ordered bougie coffee, swore every third word, and when they'd used the unisex washroom at the starport in Lisbon, he'd sat down to tinkle.

In short, it was getting really damned hard not to think of him as Chief Acquisitions Librarian Tiffany Bell right now.

Perhaps those thoughts were a little too loud.

Voice kept low but not so suspicious as a whisper, Mort leaned close. "Head in the game, kid. No time for fucking daydreaming. I've got a twist on the plan."

Oh, shit. "Um. What twist?"

"Nothing you need to worry over. Weather just gave me an idea for a bit of a distraction."

Jessie glanced up into the bright blue sky as the first hint of a reverse sunrise was fading ahead of them. They'd arrive in Boston before dawn local time, despite already seeing it from the tram depot. "There are like five clouds over the whole Atlantic. What weather?"

Mort flicked a playful finger across the tip of Jessie's borrowed nose—catching a lot less flesh than Aunt Tiffany ever did and stinging a lot less as a result. "Not your problem. What I *do* need from you is to clock that young couple in the third-egg position."

Jessie's brain freaked out a little. There was mimicking Aunt Tiffany, but this was silly. Never before—and never since

—had Jessie met anyone who described locations in a rectangular space by the relative position in a carton of a dozen eggs. This was for a great many reasons.

First, egg cartons were such a fucking mid-core grocery item. No one in the core bought livestock droppings, and the border colonies didn't use two-by-six cartons to sell them—at least not universally enough for it to be a "thing."

Second, unlike a clock, there were no established locations within the carton that corresponded to numbers. So not only would someone need to be familiar with the arrangement generally, they'd need to know specifically how Tiffany numbered them—which wasn't *that* hard, since conceptually it was squeezing the twelve clock numbers into a rectangle.

Third, you had to know the orientation. Left side, closest to the hinge, was first-egg. To Tiffany, it made intuitive sense, apparently. To anyone else, good luck.

Fourth, it was an odd, irregular application, made all the more complicated by having to transpose that carton arrangement onto beach chairs, restaurant tables, or, in this case, tram passengers.

Fifth, the entire discussion relied on both parties knowing all the aforementioned without having to go over it all, thus negating the whole point of the verbal shortcut.

Jessie *hated* the fact that she spotted Mort's intended couple instantly.

He was a twentysomething business type in a Nehru-cut suit with an immaculate pointed beard and a gleaming smile. She wore a patterned brown kerchief and carried a briefcase that screamed "defense attorney."

"I see 'em."

Mortiffany nodded. "When we exit the tram, I'm him, you're her."

"Why?"

"Just a quick delay. We'll split up and—"

"Split up?" Jessie exclaimed, fighting to keep her voice down. But her eyes shouted at her travel companion.

"It's Boston. You'll be fine. Do you know where Long Wharf is?"

"By the water?" Jessie guessed.

"You'll find it. Don't worry. Wander, though. Don't ask for directions. There's a coffee shop. You should be able to fool tech to pay using whatshername's thumb print."

Jessie stared. Eric couldn't get gross anatomical details right when cloning someone magically. Mort was confident his work could fool the Terracred Network? And for someone she doubted he'd ever met?

"And where will you be?"

"At the same cafe as you, an hour or two later."

"Care to explain why?"

"No. Just in case."

"What if something goes wrong?"

"We fix it."

"That's seriously all you can—"

"*Arriving at North Station. All passengers, please prepare to disembark.*"

Cityscape flashed past before the tram pod came to an abrupt stop that would have splattered everyone across the front windows if not for the gravity stone aboard.

Mortiffany hoisted that massive duffel bag and handed it over. Jessie grunted under the weight; it was, after all, filled with eight bowling balls and a week's worth of laundry, just to look the part of Aunt Tiffany's ubiquitous travel accessory.

Before the load put a permanent kink in Jessie's back, a hand grasped hers. The duffel became a briefcase. Jessie found herself staring through a pair of stylish-but-inert dataglasses. A quick glance revealed a change of clothing and skin tone. Her tread clacked with platform sandals obscured by her long dress.

Mort towed her off the tram pod before the other couple could reach the exit and spot them. "Cafe. Hour or two. Don't do anything rash."

The hand slipped out of Jessie's. She watched the dashing young businessman depart, wondering just what the fuck Mort was planning.

For her part, Jessie kept her feet moving, followed the traffic, and emerged outside the tram station. Following the faint whiff of saltwater in the air, she set off in search of Long Wharf and a cafe where Mort would show up within the next two hours, or Jessie was taking this plan to the next letter.

━━━

Commander Elgin Towers stood stiff and motionless as the laaku tinkered with an open panel of alien technology. None of the contents made sense to him, and he doubted the laaku engineer was going to offer tutorials willingly.

"There you go. All set," the laaku declared before levering an awkwardly large panel back into the wall and using the heel of a lower hand to bash it temporarily into staying there.

A moment later, the comm connected.

"Sir," Towers greeted the admiral with a salute.

"As you were. Status?"

"No change at this time, sir. All proceeding according to the mission directives." There was a whole coded list of ways to basically say nothing was happening while conveying a host of data back to Earth. Towers had memorized it all before departure. All of it was developed for this mission and this mission alone. Cryptography assured him that there was insufficient data for the *Arete* crew to identify patterns over the limited duration of this assignment and the expected number of communications back to Earth.

What the admiral was hearing, however, was that he and Lt. Cmdr. Kearney were being watched constantly, and the intelligence gathering had been relegated to the wizards. Not that Wizard Yarzzi would be much good on that front. The azrin was magical muscle for a ship that would be a formidable opponent in that regard. But Earth knew that as well as Towers, and the code had its limitations.

"Fine. Keep up the good work." While it was part of the return code, simple sarcasm also worked here. The admiral, though he'd never show it on a monitored comm, was furious with him. An inability to escape from surveillance and find more substantive intel on the *Arete* side *was* identified as a potential failure point for the mission, and one that Towers had assured his superiors that he could overcome.

"Thank you, sir. I look forward to our next update."

The screen went blank. The admiral knew that Towers had received his admonishment and replied with a promise to do better.

From behind him, an annoying, all-too-familiar voice snarked, "That guy even got a name?"

"He does," Towers replied tightly.

"Oi! Trebsy, get back here and yank the plug again!"

The door slid open, and the laaku engineer returned. "Shoo. Both of you. Last thing I need is an audience for the important part."

As if Towers was going to learn haathee engineering by simple observation. Even if he were to record and analyze the process, without access to an advanced engineering team back on Earth, he was unlikely to get anywhere, and he'd need that same live connection to enact repairs of his own. Basic sabotage of comms and vehicles. Installation of bugs and taps and cameras. That kind of stuff got covered in covert ops training. Unless he was to go deep undercover as a technician of some sort, that was the most Earth Navy Intelligence was going to expect of him.

And Elgin Towers's mission wasn't to break into the *Arete's* comm system. He was here to keep the crew honest and alert Earth at the first sign of treachery. Frequent, innocuous reports were his lifeline. The only time that truly mattered would be the gap between uncovering evidence of duplicity and his next arranged contact with Earth. So long as no one suspected he'd uncovered their plot, he'd have a narrow window to alert his superiors.

Failing that, he'd have a fight on his hands.

Towers exited the borrowed room, trailed by Mindy Sedgwick.

He listened, measuring the woman's pace, studiously and subtly matching the timing and length of her stride until they marched in unison. It was a deep psychological trick, one few employed. But when starting from a relationship strained by mutual orders to surveil one another, it helped to agree on the rhythm of motion, even if only one of them was aware of that accord.

"So, you order the chief engineer around. Is that it?"

"Goes both ways. We ain't beholden to ranks and chains of command to keep things running here. We's family. Commonality of purpose and all that. Where you off to, anyhow?"

"It's nearly 1900 hours. I have dinner with the captain."

"Tonight and every other night. Why you showing up this time?"

In truth, the answer was that he had found the captain infuriatingly obtuse, and her subordinates had been far more revelatory in their unguarded admissions, innocuous or not. But he was running out of leash, and when it snapped taut, Admiral Jessup would have his ass on a platter. "Oh, I suppose the war of rudeness versus my sincere desire not to disrupt operations aboard the *Arete* has finally tipped in favor of indulging Captain Ramsey this one time."

"Never picked you for a curry man."

Towers cocked his head and spared a quick glance back. "Pardon?"

"You saw the menu. That there Massaman curry what Uom'pe makes is an Earth delicacy. Had you picked for a Bratwurst fella, to be honest. Don't read nothing into that. Some of me best mates prefer raw caribou."

"Please tell me you'll be joining us this evening."

If this one had a sense of sarcasm, she hid it well. "You got an invite for 1900. I got me a night off if'n you take the captain up on it."

Towers hid his surprise. "You won't be allowed to attend?"

"Sure, if I made a stink, I prolly could. But why would I? Wait. You think just on account of I sound like this, I must be bonkers for curry?"

"No, I just—"

"Sod off. I did more growing up offworld than back home. Ate stuff you'd puke back up and asked for seconds to boot."

Much as he was tempted to toy with her verbally in an attempt to fabricate an unguarded moment, they'd reached the captain's quarters.

Sedgwick tapped the door controls and stepped aside to let him in.

Inside, a table was set taller than human standard. The reason why smashed him in the face as the other diners for the evening meal were Dr. Richelieu, who did not require such accommodation, and Grosstet, who most certainly did.

Whether the haathee was truly an ambassador of his

people... Whether he did anything to warrant the honorary rank of commodore they'd given him... He was still a hedonistic layabout with sufficient strength in that trunk of his to squeeze the flesh out of Towers's body like he was a tube of field rations.

"Commander," Captain Ramsey called out. "Didn't expect to see you here. We didn't set you a bowl."

"I SHALL BE GRACIOUS AND DONATE FROM MY OWN MEAL." While both the captain and chief medical officer had a bowl apiece before them, the haathee was arrayed with a grid of a dozen as if they were shot glasses ready for a drinking contest.

"My thanks," Towers replied as he entered. Despite the captain's protest, there was at least a seat available for him. The haathee reached out with that prodigious trunk and deftly procured a place setting's worth of flatware and a mug of beer.

A few moments later, he was legitimately enjoying the meal. Whether the tesud woman had ever set foot on Earth, she could follow a terrestrial recipe flawlessly.

"So, what made you decide to chow down with us disloyal rebels?" Ramsey asked between generous swigs of her beer. "Can't be the menu. I mean, nothing wrong with the stuff, but it's hardly on par with most of the stuff Uom'pe makes."

"Your crew is dreary company," Towers joked. He knew that playing straight with Jessica Ramsey would get him nowhere. He'd read her psych profile back to front multiple times. "I thought I'd be a bother and interfere with the ship's senior staff to discover for myself whether you'd be more engaging company."

"Ugh. Don't mention 'company' around me right now," Dr. Richelieu scolded. "I just found out today that another research site was planetized and 19 employees of mine were murdered for refusing to cooperate."

"You *did* instruct them not to do so."

"I told them to keep safe and do what they had to!"

"Words," Towers countered. "Your actions spoke differently. The message from Ghenlar Par'Mol was all too clear. Not to worry, of course. My condolences to the families, naturally, but Harmony Bay is a crucial part of the galactic economy. Once this mission is complete, and the Martian dictatorship is deposed, any and all employees and property will be returned to their rightful places."

"That wasn't my primary concern."

"It's what we can do," Captain Ramsey interjected. "We can't make meaningful changes on Mars until we clear out the squatters and return things to normal."

The haathee cocked his head. "I HAD BEEN OF THE IMPRESSION THAT EARTH WAS NOT USUALLY AN EMPIRE."

"New normal," Ramsey corrected hastily.

But it was the first chink in the armor of the *Arete's* squeaky-clean front that they were putting on for him. The haathee, Grosstet, just might be the loose-lipped informant he'd been looking for all this time.

Had it been cowardice keeping him away? One wrong word, and the elephantine giant could end his life. Ramsey was a formidable adversary. She was a certified hand-to-hand combat instructor for Earth Navy, after all, and was a highly rated operative before her disappearance. The azrin security officer could prove deadly, too, of course. But with either of those two, he had mental scenarios to defend himself, to take advantage of his surroundings or circumstances. Sneaking up on the haathee in the middle of a sound sleep, he didn't know what he'd do to the creature. All unarmed combat techniques relied on leverage, force multiplication, imbalances in soft versus hard and vital versus nonvital areas.

Grosstet's most vulnerable and sensitive areas were

impenetrable to fists and feet. His tenderest and softest flesh would be like trying to batter a punching bag.

But the mind was a weakness for all.

That was where Elgin Towers would strike. He had his target. He had his curry and beer. And he had the length of this meal to assess exactly where the haathee's vulnerabilities lay.

━━━

Pre-scripted slices of Mort. Eric served them from beneath the glass display case, where they grew crusty and stale, not fresh-from-the-oven Mortisms like Hadrian baked. But the bakery was closed, and Xilena had brought donuts from an actual patisserie that served actual food, not metaphors. Eric munched on his eighth bite-sized powdered sugar popper as Jared went over the last-minute instructions.

"We've got a nine-minute window to unload, scout the receiving dock, and return to the hovertruck. Be on the lookout for wards, sentries, or unidentified tech." The latter comment was directed to the two liaisons who'd been added to the team. Hank and Kimmie nodded their assent to the directive. Anyone else trying to follow an order to call out "unidentified tech" would have produced a list too long to be of any use.

"We should get at least one name from the dock security people," Sambrina suggested. "Make a personal connection. When we check out clean, we might receive less scrutiny on the follow-up trip."

The follow-up trip was the key. Eric had come up with some cockamamie one-two punch boxing analogy, accompanied by an anecdote about the Marquess of Queensbury. The first punch, or in this case, load of disposable party tableware, would be the initial trip. The follow-up, once they'd judged the New Vancouver Civic Arena security reality that no amount of prep could nail just right, would be the real attack.

Eric needed to delay the follow-up as long as possible. Otherwise, the plan might go off without a hitch.

Hitches were plentiful anytime Eric was involved. But something about being Mort made everything seem a little less impossible, even the stuff that really was.

Mars was at a crossroads. They were treating the upcoming election as a stamp of approval on a victory they felt they'd already won. Gathering all in one place to celebrate their political acumen and rally support for a guy projected to win approximately 110 percent of the vote was hubris. While they might not have been winning outright in the game of Battleship Bingo taking place out in the Black Ocean, they were close enough to a stalemate that a sudden swing in their fortunes seemed remote.

The Martian Circle was weak.

If Mort—the real Mort—had opted for a two-week vacation from being emperor—OK, maybe not the *real* real Mort, but the Mort that was being Khosrau at the time—he could have mopped up the rebellion without the need of a mop.

Eric, by contrast, was more bucket than mop. And he was filled with clean, soapy water. And...

"Wizard Mordecai?"

Eric blinked. He'd sidetracked himself and lost track of both the mission and where his analogy was going. "Right. We haven't got a moment to lose."

The lot of them piled into the back of a delivery hover emblazoned with a bland corporate logo and filled with stale catering smells that suggested the Martian Military Government didn't care too much for the stomachs of their supporters.

Cramped inside, it was elbows to ribs all around. Except for

Eric. Without a fingersbreadth to spare elsewhere, his co-conspirators still managed to find room enough not to come into bodily contact with him. Something about growing up with Uncle Enzio really just inured him to the horror and awe with which the rest of the magical community regarded Mordecai The Brown.

Frankly, the whole of this plan relied on that fact.

As they flew, the tech liaison pilot chattered with whoever it was who organized giant political shindigs. Eric's comrades voiced last-minute suggestions and reminders and, for a guy who really prided himself on being easygoing, started to get on his nerves.

"Shut up, the lot of you. Get in character and stay there."

He blamed his ill humor on method-acting.

Luckily, the trip was a short one.

Their delivery hover parked with a dull thud. Someone opened the doors from the outside.

"Catering for Hall J," Xilena stated brusquely to the workers running the operation at the loading dock.

"Down that corridor. Orange line on the floor."

Despite the mission, Eric found the notion of color-coded delivery help-lines delightful. It took an act of will to complain. "Yeah, yeah. This isn't the first event we've served here."

One of the problems with plans within plans was keeping straight which layer of deception was current. After all, Eric was Mordecai, and Mordecai was wearing a uniform with the name Elijah embroidered at the breast. Elijah ought to have known his business—the convention center workers needed to see that guy. And his scouting mission teammates needed to see through Elijah and see Mordecai, who was there to learn about the inner defenses of the gathering. Yet, beneath it all, Eric was supposed to be stringing this effort along without actually overthrowing anyone.

Elijah guided a trolley laden with chafing dishes.

Mordecai took note of the gentlemen with uniforms and blaster rifles.

Eric watched for excuses to call this whole thing off at the last minute.

A crackle like the calm before a thunderstorm hung in the air all around them. The Martian Circle wasn't taking their job of protecting the event from magical disturbances lightly. But the team around Eric had been assembled by The Khosrau Who Is Actually Hadrian specifically to counter those kinds of defenses.

It was all a game of chess with invisible pieces, and everyone was cheating.

"Good morning," Eric greeted the soldier who took it upon himself to follow alongside Eric's trolley at the door to Hall J.

No response met his friendly words.

That was fine. Eric had a job to do, too. His just didn't involve stomping around with a clunky blaster rifle and fifty kilos of military gear. Both, however, did their share of scowling.

The perimeter of Hall J had been devoted to refreshments. Within the surrounding tables of snacks and hors d'oeuvres, a sea of temporary chairs faced a stage festooned with Martian patriotic regalia. Flags, bunting, banners with slogans. The works.

Soldiers abounded. The officials were soldiers. The guests were soldiers. The soldiers guarding everyone were soldiers squared. Anyone not shoving around loads of food or plugging things in or straightening rows of chairs had a rank and uniform.

Even the wizards.

Mars Navy employed wizards in the same manner that Earth Navy had always done in partnership with the

Convocation. They got their medals and tassels and epaulets and snazzy dress uniform hats. But the sleeves were a little extra wide, and Eric could have spotted them without even that scant hint.

A dozen.

A score.

Eric lost count when they started entering and leaving Hall J and not wearing nametags that he could read from the catering spread.

Aside from the minor detail of an exact count, everything looked in line with the intelligence assessment prior to the mission's launch.

That was a problem.

Well, that was a problem for Eric. For Mordecai and for Elijah, everything was hunky-dory.

Eric needed something to go wrong, and the best way he could think of wasn't a Mordecai sort of solution. It was a Dad solution.

Three loads. Three round trips with the trolleys. Eric had roughly half an hour to come up with any excuse not to jump into this plan with both feet. The catering hover would be due back in two hours with a second delivery, and he had that time to throw the whole business off its orbit. But before that, he needed the plan in place to mis-spend those two hours.

Sambrina pulled the doors closed behind them.

Liaison Hank lifted them off.

Jared grinned. "That was perfect. We're ready to wreck."

"Free Mars," Xilena agreed with a grin.

Eric's Plan A had been to fake an illness. But Mordecai The Brown's reputation was such that nothing short of terminal injury would have stopped him.

Plan B was to whammy everyone and convince them to be late for the subsequent, deadlier delivery.

Plan C was to crash the delivery hover.

After a minor internal distraction, Plan D involved dinosaurs and got discarded as soon as Eric realized how far off course his mind had wandered.

Plan E was to tell the truth, and even Eric knew that was a horrible idea.

It wasn't until Plan S that Eric had a simple, obvious, workable sabotage to the mass assassination effort. He was ready before the door had shut, having come up with his line of argument on the trip back to the hover.

"You fools," Eric snapped. "You didn't feel that ward under our feet?"

"What ward?" Xilena demanded. "I didn't feel anything."

Eric harrumphed as dismissively as Ericly possible. He couldn't have harrumphed harder if he'd had actual Brown blood in his veins. "Of course, you didn't. That's why you're you and I'm still me despite being on my eighth borrowed body. I spotted it because I was *looking* for the hidden trap, not trying to confirm this information your people gathered."

"What's it do?" Jared inquired. "This ward. How is it composed?"

"Araganest's Negation, twisted with some form of crawling rune worms I'd have had to dig up the floor to examine properly. Someone in the Martian Circle has been reading naughty books. Lucky for you people, I'm extremely well read."

"What can we do about it?"

"We need backup. Liaison Kimmie, when we're able, contact Earth and get us backup. I'll need a rune-breaker team and someone skilled in moving large amounts of rock and soil as quietly as possible. And if we can get them here in the next five or so hours, we'll still be able to pull off this coup before the delegates and officials scatter back to the twenty corners of Mars."

That pronouncement kicked off a minor frenzy.

Eric sat back and let the chaos unfold.

It was an Emperor's New Clothes scam. Dad always said never to believe anyone who claimed to see things you couldn't. But with wizards, grains of salt came with their own grains of salt. Not being able to see what others could was a major insecurity among the lesser rungs of the Convocation ladder. Special insights. Forbidden knowledge. Wizards ate that stuff up. Eric himself had always been particularly vulnerable to that foible. But he also had a habit of seeing things where and when he needed to see them, whether or not they were the *right* things.

Now, he'd turned that weakness on its head.

He'd bought the Earth coup time.

It was up to Mort (the real Mort who looked like Hadrian) and Jessie now to finish things.

Emperor Khosrau Blackstone drummed his fingers on the armrest of his throne. These were two habits he'd adopted in this guise. Nervous fidgeting, especially with the fingers, was rare in successful wizards, but after coaching on the former occupant's mannerisms, Hadrian found that the quirk had taken hold of him like a tick. Sitting on thrones, as a rule, was reserved for those with subjects to rule and was even less common.

Only Vincente was around to witness this unique combination. Wasted effort acting in front of one of the few who knew his secret.

"And they're requesting additional support to complete the mission," the emperor's chief adviser reported. "Magical demolition and an oracle well versed in wards."

"Which means precisely what?" Khosrau demanded. This was the stupid shit he'd feared when trying to blackmail his grandfather. Foot dragging. Excuses. Petty annoyances. Wheedling.

"We have a window of four and a half hours to get the necessary support to the team in New Vancouver. Wizard Mordecai believes they will have a better chance of success but will still make an attempt if we are unable to comply with his request."

Fingers continued to drum. Four beats, four beats, four beats. Like a horse's gallop. Like a monk's chant. The rhythm lulled his thoughts and distracted his focus.

"Fine. Send whatever they need." Khosrau flung a hand with a flick of his wrist.

Vincente bowed. "Due to the urgent nature of the missive, I took the liberty before informing you. The reinforcements could have been recalled had you deemed the request inadvisable."

Khosrau gritted his teeth. Would he? Would Vincente have recalled the demolition squad? Or would the shrewd wizard have merely compounded the deception one level deeper?

"Is that all?" the emperor snapped. He intended to head straight to the harem after this.

"I actually have better news, Your Majesty," Vincente replied with a smile. "Per your request, Wizard Tiffany has arrived back on Earth."

Khosrau grunted. "About time."

"Shall I have her brought to the palace?"

Timing was crucial. Missteps could be costly. Wizard Tiffany was a wild card; she knew his identity and supported him for the good of humankind, not for his politics, and certainly not for any friendship or affection. Handling her was more art than magic. In his current state of pique, he'd risk angering her. And much as she'd grudgingly accepted the reality of imperial succession as a volume industry, meeting with her smelling of the affections of half a dozen concubines would be certain to draw her ire and distract from any meaningful interaction.

Khosrau needed time to sate his loins, calm his worries, bathe, and change clothes. That said, time was pressing on him.

How did one relax in a hurry?

"Three hours, rounded up."

"She's not known for her patience..."

No. But Wizard Tiffany had predilections of her own. "Do we still have that young courier from the Order of Hermes on staff?"

"The one with the disproportionate—?"

"Yes," Khosrau cut in. He'd heard Wizard Tiffany's crude assessment of the young man's anatomy. "Send the good librarian a bottle of something expensive and make sure he's the one to deliver it. We'll be *lucky* if she makes it here in three hours."

"Very good, Sire."

Vincente bowed lower and excused himself from the imperial presence.

Alone in his throne room, Khosrau stewed.

The stakes were too high. In five hours, Mars would be in chaos. Within a week, he could be accepting the fealty of the red planet on behalf of some middling functionary pressed into the role of interim dictator. Before month's end, he could be the undisputed monarch of all humanity.

Infants in the nursery would one day vie for the throne upon which he presently sat. His name would echo down the halls of history. And yet, one wrong step, one wrong word to the wrong person at the wrong time would send him crashing into ruin.

A professional juggler could keep five or six balls in the air with ease. Khosrau had lost count of his, and he relied far too heavily on Vincente to keep them aloft.

Springing from his throne, Khosrau resolved to press forward. Exiting through the private doors to his personal quarters, he headed for his harem—his sanctuary.

"Shall I prepare your evening's diversion?" Katarina queried, catching him just on the far side of the throne room door as the women of his personal guard detail fell in to escort them. The overseer of his harem was nothing if not attentive.

"Whoever's next. I have a meeting in three hours and I'll need to be freshened up by then."

"Of course, Your Majesty," Katarina replied with a quick nod. On slippered feet that made only a whisper on the floor tile, she hurried ahead of him.

Mind still yet to be calmed, racing thoughts outpaced them both. "And send someone to check on Ramsey. Make sure he's enjoying his stay with us."

Katarina whirled, backing away down the corridor with another bow. "Of course. I know just whom to assign."

Good. One more ball he wouldn't bobble before his master plan came to fruition. The last thing he needed was Carl Ramsey bitching to Wizard Mordecai about his ill-treatment.

━━

Carl caught a grape in his mouth. Grapes were on a short list of foods that were more fun than flavor. Every bunch was a carnival game disguised as a snack. It had been Ozzy who'd been big on them as a kid, and the floor of the *Mobius* had been sticky with homemade grape juice for months thanks to how often the little treats missed his mouth and got stepped on.

These days, he was only missing one out of every five or six grapes, and some palace maid ensured that any messes were tidied before they became endemic. During the brief chew before swallowing, Carl resumed strumming chords.

"It sounds familiar, but I can't place it," his guest told him.

Hesperia plucked another grape and lobbed it his way. When the emperor's people had relented and sent one of the concubines his way, Carl could only marvel at their sense of humor and take the "gift" in stride. A good eight months pregnant and eager to collapse into the room's most comfortable chair immediately upon arrival, she was hardly in any state for hanky panky. And as a middling wizard herself, she was in no real danger from a geriatric rock musician if he had any ideas about hostages.

"Original composition," Carl claimed, though he was getting the same vibe as he strummed and was thinking it sounded a little Led Zeppelin. "You like it?"

"Very much," Hesperia replied, and Carl couldn't tell whether she was being polite or obsequious. After all, if she was here to keep up his spirits, shitting on his music wasn't going to win her any points.

Fingering his way through a riff his hands knew without guidance, he shifted the subject. "So, what got you kicked out of paradise today?"

She shrugged, shifting a purple silk robe that was apparently the most clothing she or her colleagues ever wore these days. "Bringing down the lustful aesthetic, I suppose." Hesperia's smile hid something. Pain of rejection, maybe. Mourning a loss of status, perhaps. She'd admitted on a previous visit that the emperor only knew the names of his wives, not the concubines who filled out the ranks of his personal playground. Life as an anonymous heir incubator couldn't be great for the self-esteem.

A flat palm stilled the guitar's strings. "That's what I don't get. The whole underlying deal of heterosexuality is kids. It's all fun and games until someone gets knocked up. Then you get to sit back and enjoy a break."

"*You* get a break. Not your wife."

"C'mon. She didn't lift a finger while the kids were baking. I treated her like a princess."

"I'm no princess," Hesperia reminded him.

Carl shot her a lopsided grin. "I'm no emperor. Hey, if Amy brought in a bunch of friends while she was pregnant with Jessie, I wouldn't have sent her away."

"How magnanimous," his guest teased. She tossed him another grape, but Carl caught this one with his hand and set it on the table beside his easy chair.

"No. I'm serious. I'm not saying to *confront* the guy or anything. Maybe just... make it clear that he can be proud of you and that's OK."

"He sends me to make sure *you're* happy, you know."

Carl chuckled. "But only to a degree. Right?"

She nodded toward the instrument resting on his lap. "Pick up that guitar and prove you're not enjoying this."

Carl crossed his legs beneath the instrument. "Not the point."

"He needs to blow off steam. The kind that produces more heirs. I'm just one of the ones in the way of that."

"I get the fun part of the whole deal. But blowing off steam? The guy literally has people to run the empire for him. All he's got is leisure time plus what agendas he wants to push as a hobby. What could possibly stress him out?"

"Oh. You know. Emperor stuff. Certain people."

"Give it a rest," Carl countered. "You ladies spend all day gossiping with the guards and servants when he's not around. You know everything that goes on around here. Who's got him riled up? Is it that skinny dude with the accent?"

"Vincente? No. Hardly. Vincente's the only one other than us who seems to reassure him."

"Oh *really*?"

"Not that way!" Hesperia protested with a giggle. "He's just... competent. Not that his evening guest isn't. But she's—"

"Aha! It's a *she*!"

"Fine. Wizard Tiffany. She'd make anyone uncomfortable."

"You've met her?"

"No, thank Hera! She won't set foot in the harem despite Emperor Khosrau offering an exemption to the dress code."

"Yeah. Can't see him enforcing that one. She's a little shit, but she's always been a handful. Learned magic from a friend of mine, if you can believe it."

"Mister Ramsey—"

"Carl. I keep telling you."

"*Mister* Ramsey, if Miss Katarina warned of one thing before sending me here, it was that no one can believe *anything* you say."

A couple quick raps at the door were a well-known signal.

Carl set down the guitar and hopped to his feet as best he could. Offering a hand, he helped Hesperia get up from the cushioned luxury of her chair.

Bare feet slapped on the cold floor. She leaned on him for balance the first few steps. She slipped free and made the rest of her way solo. The door opened. She slipped through. A hand reached back and hung a flimsy purple robe on a hook just Carl's side of the door. The footsteps resumed on the far side just before the door shut once more.

Tiffany Bell.

A chance?

An opportunity?

Carl's mind whirled with possibilities. He wouldn't have counted the visit any more of a success if that robe and

Hesperia had ended up with their places reversed on opposite sides of that door.

━━━

Charlotte had switched up the babysitting teams' assignments. Daphne found herself monitoring Elgin Towers over dinner. The man was loathsome, all the more so for appearing too outwardly dignified and refined.

The Earth Navy Intelligence officer sipped nonalcoholic wine with the flute pinched delicately between finger and thumb. He nibbled mincing bites of well-done steak doused in ketchup. He sprinkled so much black pepper in his soup that it changed color. Between morsels, he daubed at the corner of his mouth with a napkin.

"You're welcome to join me," the commander teased.

"I ate," Daphne replied.

"Wizard Yarzzi has been asking about you, you know. If you'd rather dine with *him*, I'd entirely understand."

"I ate already," Daphne reiterated.

"A dessert, perhaps, then?"

Dessert wasn't an azrin cultural concept. Daphne enjoyed a good ice cream sundae as much as the next Toronto Prime girl, but from the smell of his breath, Yarzzi liked his meat bloody and followed by a second helping of raw animal flesh, not sweet frozen treats.

"You can pass along my regrets. He's not my type."

Towers emitted a single, self-amused chuckle. "Oh, I think once the assignment is over, he wasn't planning on asking permission."

Daphne's fur stood on end at the back of her neck. Even among her Meyang brethren, such acts were more a courtship pantomime than actual mating practices. A nice azrin girl was supposed to *want* to get thrown around, maybe bitten or clawed a little, but only by her chosen suitor. Daphne and the azrin wizard had crossed paths, and unless his magic was going to make the difference, she couldn't picture him winning a wrestling match she had no intention of throwing.

The human was just trying to get under her skin. To throw her off her game. Daphne refused to let the tactic work.

"Just a friendly reminder that you're still guests on our ship. Once this mission is over, you go home."

"Ah, yes. The utter confidence that your wizard friend will both keep up his end of the emperor's bargain *and* pull off a galactic-scale coup. I do hope for your sake that this all goes according to plan."

"I think it's you who'd better hope," Daphne countered, hackles still up. "Eric Ramsey is stronger than you realize."

"Oh. I'd almost forgotten. You've done such an excellent job of keeping him hidden away that I'd almost forgotten he was even around here. Somewhere. Yarzzi hasn't even caught a whiff of him. Lt. Cmdr. Kearney is quite smitten with his dossier picture. Be a shame if she didn't at least get a chance to meet him before we depart."

"I'll see what I can arrange," Daphne grumbled. She fought back the impulse to narrow her eyes in a glare. But her suspicions were growing. They were ready to bloom. "Can I trust you to remain in the dining lounge a moment?"

"Of course," the commander answered without the faintest hesitation.

Daphne excused herself with a nod and headed into the corridor. Once the door slid shut behind her, she burst into a sprint for the nearest lift.

"Bridge."

The ride lasted seconds in which she aged years.

When the *Arete's* command center opened before her, Daphne raced to the command chair. "Captain!"

Charlotte turned her way wearing Captain Ramsey's body and face. "What is it, Lt. Morgan?"

"I think they know. Not *know* know, but they at least strongly suspect that Eric isn't aboard the *Arete*."

"Do they have a theory as to his whereabouts?"

Even in a growing, contagious panic, Daphne knew the question didn't sound like anything the captain would say despite the voice matching Jessie's. "It was only a hint. I'm not even sure they're sure. But they're preparing themselves for the mission's failure, and I don't think they're planning to go away quietly."

Daphne didn't have to say it out loud. Towers and Kearney were mere humans. Adept intelligence officers, but with the H-tech systems all around them, there was little chance of hacking or sabotage, and in a military engagement, the *Arete* crew would deal with them handily. But Wizard Cornelius was a fleet wizard and Wizard Yarzzi a prodigy.

And the *Arete* only had Charlotte and Sparta to counter them.

"Where did you leave your subject?"

"He's finishing dinner. Uom'pe will keep an eye."

"Find him. Take him into custody. Make sure *all* comms are shut down."

"But what if—"

"We cannot take that chance!" Charlotte snapped. "We can't put the ship on alert, but spread the word silently. Our only hope is to catch them one by one without them realizing the others have been taken. Understood?"

Daphne swallowed. "Yes, ma'am."

Sparta watched the stars. While they couldn't convey prophecy in their errant arrangement, they were both pretty and comforting. A billion planets orbited in uncaring mathematical perfection without a concern for the machinations of tiny animal lives. One day, she would be dust in that cosmos. It was the meantime that weighed on her mind.

For most of her life, the future had been a well-paved path. Ankle-high decorative fencing and little signs warning her to Keep Off the Grass had been all it took for her to see a destination clearly and know where she would be.

St. Albans prep school on scholarship she'd told her mother to apply for.

She'd shared her first kiss with Manuel Ramos, knowing his father would be reassigned in a week and he'd never write to her.

A letter of acceptance to Oxford and her own letter requesting a recommendation from the Undersecretary of Recruitment for the Order of Delphi crossed in the mail.

She guessed at answers to questions she hadn't studied and aced exams.

When offered the teaching assistant position prior to starting her master's degree, she'd been carrying a box with personal effects for her office.

The fates of others required but a little attention and a quiet mind.

Until Mordecai.

She'd met him standing on the paved path through life, and he'd beckoned for her to follow him onto the forbidden grass. The sheer novelty of a man who controlled a fate she couldn't see gained her attention until she fell in love with a force of nature itself. Now, she wished she could glimpse just enough of his future to know that Mordecai was all right.

Even her own future had grown murky. Around Mordecai,

she was adrift in a bubble of agency that destiny couldn't penetrate. Eric operated in a bubble of his own. Jessica and Carl likewise inherited Mordecai's resistance to the pull of fate's current.

She could find no answers in the stars. Without a stellar cartographer's help, she couldn't even tell which bright dot might have been Sol.

Her precognition wasn't so atrophied that Sparta didn't whirl a second before her door burst open without so much as a knock.

Jessica Ramsey blew in like a sirocco wind. Of course, Sparta saw the fingerprints of Mordecai's magic all over the disguise and knew in an instant that this was Wizard Charlotte. "We've a problem of the most urgent sort."

"Someone slipped up?" There was only one threat to the *Arete* at present. Their guests were sizzling fuses of unknown length. Sooner or later, they were bound to reach the end of their ropes.

"Possibly. I've shut down comms and the hangar. Lifts are offline until further notice."

"But won't they—?"

"Yes," Charlotte snapped. "But the alternative was allowing them to rally and strike as a combined force. Our only hope is to confront them separately."

"Confront?" Sparta echoed incredulously. "No offense, but I don't stand a chance against those wizards in a fight, and you barely tip the scales. Either of them would overpower us both with ease."

Charlotte marched up to her. In Jessica's uniformed body, she was forced to crane her neck to look Sparta in the eye. It was perhaps the most damning testament to the pirate progeny's lack of power that a mere oracle was willing to meet that Morphean gaze.

"Look here. Mordecai The Brown isn't the sort to have left his paramour undefended. He must have left you protections."

"Yes, but—"

"If ifs and buts were candy and nuts... We can't afford to be taken on defense. We must strike first or perish."

Sparta gulped. This was it. This was the "adventure" Mordecai had promised. The sudden premonition of death, so clear that even non-oracles would see it in the room with them. Life hanging by a thread of wit and willpower alone.

She couldn't hesitate any longer. Mordecai would either be proud of Sparta or mourn her.

Blustering past Charlotte, Sparta flung open a dresser drawer and rummaged until she came away with a small book in her hand.

"What's that?" the *Arete's* interim captain demanded.

"I'm... not entirely sure. Mordecai warded it shut." Sparta held up the miniature tome and waggled it to show off a gold clasp, locked tight.

"You have the key?"

"No."

"Then what good is it?"

"He said it wasn't for me to open."

Charlotte recoiled from it. "Well, if you can't, then I certainly won't be able to."

"It's a trap. That much I know. It wouldn't go well for anyone breaking it open."

"He left that around the ship, Eric being Eric?"

Sparta cracked a tiny smile. "I asked the same thing. He said Eric would be fine. But I doubt the wizards we've got around here would be so fortunate."

Charlotte shook her head. "I'm not sure I like the Poisoned Cookie as our plan of attack."

Like Sparta did? This was an act of desperation. "Then

maybe we should have killed our guests *before* they got suspicious."

Sparta couldn't believe her own ears. It was as if Mordecai's pragmatic bloodlust had rubbed off on her.

Or perhaps she'd just found a new path, one trampled through the grass and unmarked, clear to her eyes for the first time.

⬜▭

Eric wasn't honestly sure what he'd have done if Earth had refused to send more people to help with his plan. There was just a way things like this were done. An urgent mission needed backup, and they got it. There was never a "well, we'll try again next year" or a shrug and a "do your best" pep talk.

The catering crew was back and preparing for the post-rally feast. This was their last chance with everybody all rounded up together. Hank and Kimmie kept earpieces hidden away under company hats that everyone wore. Newcomers hadn't fit in with the whole "we're here to deliver food" excuse for being here. No catering company suddenly needed twice as many employees to lug the same amount of food.

Eric pushed his hover trolley, careful not to do anything that might splutter out its hovery bits and crash it. Meanwhile, the others had the wary looks of people who knew they stood poised on the diving board of history while someone filled the pool from a garden hose.

"Copy that," Kimmie muttered into her shirt collar. The six of them were halfway down a corridor, between guard stations. She shot a glare back at Eric, voice low but overflowing with frustration. "Basement team isn't finding anything."

"Tell them to keep looking," Eric retorted.

"They are," Kimmie assured him. The others guided their

trolleys, eavesdropping openly. "How sure are you that there wasn't a trick to make you *think* you saw a—"

"I know what I felt." Eric wasn't going to let a liaison second-guess him, even if she was completely right. It wasn't just un-Mordecai-like, it ran counter to his whole distraction plan.

One major flaw in the whole operation, as he saw it, was getting word back from Earth that Dad was safe and he could stop pretending to be someone he wasn't qualified to impersonate beyond a certain point.

Bluster. Bully. Badger. Eric could fake all that. He could manage enough magic that no one would ever consider that he wasn't a wizard—or even an overqualified underachiever without a right to the actual title of wizard. But if the Martians decided they weren't on the up and up, or the Earthlings figured out that he wasn't playing for their team, either, Eric could have been in a lot of trouble.

In fact, Eric could have accidentally brokered a nice little truce between the two sides he was simultaneously betraying.

"Time to split up," Xilena reminded them all as they approached the convention floor doors.

Each of them ferried snacks for a different section of Hall J. A table of salty foods here. Dips and veggies there. A buffet of cookies. Coolers of prepackaged ice cream cups. Eric's had a cake with a Martian flag on it, pre-cut into 120 slices.

If Eric was going to take out his escort, now was the time. His last chance to have them all clustered together.

All he had to do was...

It was too late.

Killing, incapacitating, or otherwise rendering his co-conspirators no continued threat to Martian security passed him by as the trolleys exited into the convention hall where deafening cheers and science-amplified speeches assailed the ears.

There hadn't been a lot of time for new plans.

Under New Vancouver Civic Arena, the new additions to the team were supposed to take out the ward protecting the place. Eric, as Mordecai The Brown, was supposed to have been perceptive enough to tell when they'd finished their work. His job was to incinerate everyone in Hall J while Jared, Sambrina, and Xilena prevented anyone escaping, and Hank and Kimmie secured their getaway.

As a lifelong planner, Eric found the whole operation very Plan A–centric.

"Hey..."

Eric ignored the voice. He had a mission, and he wasn't supposed to consort with the guests.

"HEY!"

Uh-oh. That was directed his way.

Glancing up from his work, Eric caught sight of a dossier staring his way.

Vice Admiral Jenneth Bronson. Commander of the Martian 4th Fleet. Eighteenth in line for leadership of Mars. "Just what do you think you're doing?"

Eric considered a myriad snarky, truthful, and pre-prepared answers to that question before settling on "My job."

"You've got the goddamn cake upside down!"

Eric took a quick glance to double-check. No. He had it frosting-side up. "I hate to argue with a guest, but I've got it the right way."

Two hands moved quicker than Eric was expecting. One lasered a finger toward the stage, festooned with Martian patriotic regalia. The other drew a blaster sidearm and aimed it toward Eric. "A thousand fucking flags in the room, and you can't even check? What kind of Earthling spy are you?"

The man was clearly drunk, both from the flush of his face and his slurred words. Now that Eric looked more closely, however, the guy had a point. Eric had oriented the flag so that it looked right from his side, not the side where partygoers would file past to take a slice.

But drunk or not, the accusation hit a mark that wouldn't be cleared simply by pointing out that a three-star Mars Navy Admiral had a few too many cups of spiked punch that evening.

The two made eye contact.

Eric found himself in a War Room. Dim lights. Blinky panels. Officers in headsets manning important-looking stations. All the male officers were square-jawed and clean cut, brawny and steely-eyed. The women were... well, Eric wasn't here to judge, but it was clear that Admiral Bronson had his ideas of the role of gender in his navy.

"What the HELL are you doing here?" the admiral demanded.

"Sorry. The Earth spy thing was too good a guess. Not your lucky day. Don't worry, this is only going to *look* like I'm killing you."

"WHAT?"

But it was already too late for Jenneth Bronson, formerly a vice admiral in Mars Navy.

Eric blinked and found himself staring at a blank-faced youth from across a flag cake facing the wrong direction. And from *this* side of the table, that flag was clearly upside down. But it was *his* hand holding the blaster, and Eric had already evacuated this body's resident.

"There's a traitor here, but it's not you!" he announced as the crowd buzzed, wondering what to do about a senior officer holding a caterer at blasterpoint.

Eric resolved to end the standoff as quickly as feasible.

He aimed the blaster at the side of his head and squeezed the trigger. However, thanks to self-preservation instincts, he ducked at the last second, firing over his own borrowed head.

Conventioneers screamed. Armed officers drew weapons of their own. Noncommissioned soldiers swarmed in to take custody of the weapon away from Eric before he hurt himself or someone else.

It took two more shots before Eric managed to hit the admiral.

Suddenly, with a quick wave of vertigo, Eric was back in his own body, being jostled as the emergency response flooded past.

Someone grabbed him by the arm with a hand like a vise. "You'll need to come with me."

Eric needed no such thing.

His benign assailant could try grabbing him again tomorrow. The soldier vanished into the fourth dimension.

Stumbling and pushing ineffectually against the flow of curious Martian military personnel, Eric fled Hall J of the New Vancouver Civic Arena.

Jessie's borrowed skin crawled. Boston Prime was enemy territory. No. Not *just* enemy territory; this was the heart of the corrupt empire that had fractured ARGO and pitted Earth and Mars against one another. It was also where Emperor Khosrau was holding Carl hostage.

Hadrian.

The body-swapping still messed with her head. Hadrian's body belonged to Uncle Enzio now. Uncle Enzio, who'd been Mordecai The Brown all along. She was pushing aside the fact that *he* was the one who founded this empire for the time being. It was the real Hadrian The Brown, inhabiting Khosrau Blackstone's body, who'd taken her father prisoner.

But the body-swapping hadn't ended there. Mort was still walking around looking like Aunt Tiffany. An uncanny likeness even Jessie couldn't see past.

"Oh, just fucking pretend you've been here before," Mortiffany snapped. "You're embarrassing us both."

"Sorry," Jessie replied, bowing her head in mock contrition.

"Emperor wanted to see me," Mort told the guards at the palace gates. They didn't so much as lift a finger to slow her progress. No one questioned a companion of Aunt Tiffany's. It was continuing to dawn on Jessie just how the rest of the galaxy regarded some of the Ramseys' oldest family friends.

Jessie craned her neck, watching the darkening skies as storm clouds formed high above the palace grounds. "I thought Earth didn't get unauthorized weather."

"It happens occasionally."

"How occasionally?" Jessie pressed.

"About as often as I run errands on the way to a palace summons," Mort replied cryptically.

He'd yet to reveal any details about his side excursion. Given the nature of their mission, idle shopping or social calls seemed unlikely. But what it *had* been continued to elude her.

The palace itself was old school Earth architecture, all stonework and empty space. Guards deferred to them at every turn. And while Jessie had only studied the building from computerized maps, she was certain this wasn't the way to go snooping around for the guest quarters where Carl was likely being held.

"Where. Are. We. Going?" she demanded through gritted teeth, aware that the walls had ears both technological and likely magical.

"To put a stop to this."

Jessie's feet kept moving, but her heart plopped out and splattered to the floor behind them. No... He couldn't be jettisoning their already-risky plan. Get in. Grab Carl. *Then* deal with Khosrau.

No objection she could dare voice would have done anything to improve their chances of success. Confront Mort here and now, and they'd alert the palace guards and whoever else might be around to cause them trouble. Even if he relented, the damage would be done. All she could do was hang on and hope the coming plunge was more roller coaster than waterfall.

More guards opened the doors to the Imperial Throne Room. As soon as they had a line of sight to the throne itself, the gaudy chair's occupant greeted them.

"Ah. There you are. It's about time."

Though the voice was that of the emperor, Jessie forced her ear to hear the words as Hadrian's. This was still the same snotty kid that Harmony had knocked around in the inaugural Arete Games.

Mort entered as Tiffany Bell. Courtiers lingering in the throne room cast their eyes upon the familiar visitor to the palace, and a few even spared a quick glance at the librarian's companion, only adding to Jessie's unease.

"Well, I'm here now. You're welcome."

"Someone *please* tell me I don't fucking sound like that."

Jessie froze to the floor. That voice. Mort had it perfect, but this was the original. From a shadowed corner of the throne room, Aunt Tiffany stepped into view.

Mort didn't so much as break stride as he continued toward the dais upon which the throne rested.

Jessie scanned the crowd. This wasn't the usual assemblage of politicians and sycophants she'd have suspected. Many bore faces she knew from newsfeeds. Others simply bore a look that screamed their profession. Wizards. Wizards everywhere.

They'd walked into a trap.

"I see we have a surplus of foul-tempered librarians," Emperor Khosrau joked, grinning for sport.

"What's even in that bag?" Aunt Tiffany inquired loudly enough for all to hear.

Mort shrugged, still using the librarian's visage. "Three days' laundry, a few hardbound books, snacks, and seven human skulls."

"WHAT?" Jessie couldn't help exclaiming. She had never dared look inside Aunt Tiffany's duffel bag, thanks to certain creative threats from the owner, and somehow that reluctance had carried over to its fake counterpart.

Aunt Tiffany merely smirked behind those crystal spectacles of hers. "Just seven?"

However, the emperor wasn't about to let his spotlight be stolen away. "Mordecai, I'd hoped for better from you. Did your friend's life mean that little? Or were you just so brazen that you expected to march in here and bully me into returning him?"

Jessie's mind whirled. This was a tactical situation on a plane she couldn't comprehend. So many wizards. So many enemies of unknown power and skill. At her side, the fake Tiffany Bell melted back into Hadrian's form, but it was Mort at her side. She didn't know how strong he was, either. Just that he was more powerful than any of these Earthling conjurers. Everyone said so.

The disguise around Jessie faded as well, leaving her exposed, outed, revealed as a traitor and conspirator against her rightful emperor. There was no turning back from this. Public execution or private, she was a dead woman if they didn't find a way out of this. And fast.

The elder wizard didn't turn her way, but the soft-spoken

words were for Jessie alone. "Relax. We still have the upper hand."

———

Back aboard the *Arete*, the search was underway. Word of mouth had spread like an electrical storm through the ship's systems. Daphne retraced her steps, only to find that Towers was gone from the dining lounge.

A quick sniff nearly cost the azrin security officer a lung. Acrid, invisible vapor hung in the air, burning sensitive nostrils and causing a spasm and cough that saved her from worse harm. Covering her face with a hand, she scrambled for the exit before a gut-wrenching realization.

Uom'pe!

Taking as deep a breath as her stinging lungs could stand, she held her breath and ventured back inside.

In the kitchen, she found the tesud on the floor, a blaster hole through her shell. Maybe tesud anatomy wasn't a strong subject for the Earthling spy, but Towers had missed the heart. Daphne attempted to check for a pulse only to realize that she knew just as little about chelonian physiology.

Regardless of species, there had to be blood flowing to her head, and tesuds *did* have hearts. Daphne held a palm to the side of Uom'pe's neck and... nothing.

Feeling dizzy, needing a breath, yet unwilling to risk the air in the kitchen or dining lounge, Daphne first thought to haul Uom'pe out of the area, then realized she'd pass out before getting the tesud cook's considerable mass out to the corridor. Scanning the area, she found a solution.

The stovetop burners were hot, but Daphne leaned over them anyway, using the sleeve of her uniform to shield her as she sucked in a breath from beneath the aftermarket vent hood the engineering staff had installed for human-style cooking aboard the *Arete*. Four full breaths, raw and painful, and she had the strength to hold one lungful and drag Uom'pe out of the kitchen.

Groggy eyes opened a crack.

"G.o. I. Wi.ll. B.e. F.i…"

Daphne opened a comm. "Med Bay. Uom'pe is down. Outside the dining lounge. Towers shot her. I'm in pursuit."

"*Copy that,*" Dr. Richelieu responded. "*On my way.*"

"*Since we're sayin' sod it about the comm silence, I put a hole in Kearney,*" Mindy reported in. "*Well, two if'n we're bein' technical. Weren't takin' no chances.*"

With her nose in no fit shape for tracking, the hunt would be a battle of wits. Towers was Daphne's problem. She owed it to Uom'pe to catch him before anyone else got hurt.

Thanks to her H-tech upgrades, Daphne liked her odds.

As soon as the comm ended, Harmony sprang into action. Under normal circumstances, injured crew would be rushed to Med Bay, where a whole host of emergency options stood ready at the doctor's disposal. However, this being a pseudo-military vessel, not every life-threatening injury could be whisked to her doorstep like an order from Comet Pizza.

Right outside the entrance to Med Bay, a field kit contained everything she'd need to stabilize a trauma victim suffering anything short of vaporization.

Uom'pe…

Stupid, harmless old turtle! What business did she have getting in the way of violence? Didn't two centuries of questionable dealings teach her when to tuck her head inside her shell? Figuratively, of course. Anatomically, Harmony knew that tesuds couldn't manage that trick.

Her own whirling thoughts caught on a snag and snapped to a halt when the Med Bay door opened before its standard auto-trigger range, revealing one of the Earthling guests.

"Excuse me, I'm needed on an urgent matter that—"

Harmony's voice caught in her chest as a suffocating force gripped her entire body. Wizard Cornelius had an expressionless face, aside from the fire in his eyes. "You will be allowed to move in a moment. Upon your limited release, you will gather the most valuable of your scientific artifacts and turn them over to me. You will then accompany my companions and myself to our conveyance and onward to Earth. In exchange for your cooperation, you will be treated well and released upon our arrival on Earth. As a Martian traitor, we have no quarrel with you. I'm going to allow you to speak. I'd like you to confirm your understanding of the circumstances."

Fury boiled inside Harmony Richelieu. How *dare* he? The magical grasp was so tight that her lungs couldn't expand. In a lesser creature, the imminent threat of suffocation would induce panic. Adrenal release. Impaired reasoning. Agreement to any terms that promised continued survival.

But Harmony's lungs weren't starved for oxygen. H-tech drones transported oxygen to the blood without the lungs needing to act, pumped that blood without the need of heart contractions. Surely, she'd have been better off with those drones performing more advanced structural and cellular work, but Protocol 97 kicked in without her needing to enact it manually.

The magical stranglehold eased. Harmony nodded. "I understand the circumstances just fine."

Wizard Cornelius gave a curt nod. "Good."

Harmony could move once more. But he hadn't released her yet. The *Arete's* chief medical officer dissected the man in her mind's eye. Her own keen visual swept him with diagnostic attention to detail.

Unnatural pallor for a planetsider indicated a mild case of anemia.

The squint of his eyes suggested untreated myopia.

The particular stink of his breath indicated gum disease.

None of these observations suggested in any way that a sudden aneurysm or stroke might save her from a confrontation. But the imperfections warred with the man's self-image as a self-important magical conduit to forces beyond scientific comprehension.

Science comprehended this doughy, sickly, narcissist just fine.

Low muscle tone.

Dry skin.

Patchy beard disguised with cosmetic oils.

Slightly crooked teeth that no one probably dared to complain about to his face.

This was a human who kept himself alive in defiance of modern medicine.

Today, modern medicine was defying him right back.

This collection of molecules and neuroelectric signals had chosen the wrong hostage.

Harmony's fist broke the wizard's concentration, sending him staggering to the wall with a bloody nose. A clawed hand came up and aimed her way, but the lights in Med Bay didn't so much as blink.

Equations, molecular diagrams, and biodynamic models swam in Harmony's mind. She pictured the cartilage she'd fractured, listed the capillaries that had broken, calculated the projected rate of coagulation of the blood spewing from the wound.

Unsure how long she could keep such a stringent focus, Harmony closed in.

Stronger, faster, moderately skilled, her opponent was a head taller and twice her mass, not to mention panicked. She struck him a glancing blow to the jaw but ended up wrapped in a bear hug and rammed against the Med Bay wall in the ensuing scuffle.

Unable to overcome both her opponent's bulk and adrenaline-fueled strength at once, she turned her disadvantage in height to her advantage. Rising on her toes, she cracked the crown of her head into Wizard Cornelius's chin.

The man stumbled away from her.

Wizards, not known for either their stupidity or their bravery, turned for the door and ran.

The door opened at his approach, which wasn't usually the case for wizards. In much the way that cameras failed to capture their image, most automated doors couldn't tell they were there. Generally, the Med Bay autodoors were no exception.

But it wasn't a sudden burst of insight from the doors that had convinced them to open.

Medic Daschel was on the far side of that door. Similar in size, her bulk leaned toward brawn whereas Wizard Cornelius had a decided bent toward flab. The wizard struck a stiffened arm that came up and stopped the wizard comically in his tracks.

Whether by instinct or intent, Britney Daschel wasn't content merely to impede the wizard's egress from Med Bay. Cornelius's lower body carried forward as Britney's blow lifted him from the floor by his sternum.

A terrified wheeze escaped as the breath was driven from the wizard's lungs.

Stepping into the attack, Britney took control of one flailing arm and piloted the wizard to the floor with both his weight and hers behind the blow.

A terrible crack caused a wince as the wizard landed skull first. In her state of hyperawareness, Harmony envisioned in gruesome detail the spiderweb shattering of parietal and occipital bones.

Blood and brain matter splashed from the site. More blood continued to pool as the pair stood over the body.

"Sorry," Britney muttered. "I know. Do no harm."

Harmony shuffled around the growing pool and retrieved the emergency med kit. Not for Wizard Cornelius, of course. There was still a tesud chef out there who'd gotten herself shot and was probably exhausting her limited supply of haathee drones.

The doctor shook her head at the spy on her floor. "Forget about it. He was like this when we found him."

"Yes, Doctor," Britney replied with a dutiful nod before falling in and following Harmony toward the dining lounge.

⊏⊐

"Do you really think I can't hear you whispering over there?" Khosrau taunted.

"Didn't really care one way or the other," Mort replied casually.

The audience murmured amongst themselves briefly before the emperor silenced them with a raised hand. "You may be mighty. Mightier than any of us, even. But you won't be able to light so much as a birthday candle with all of us opposing you."

Mort harrumphed. "Not going to be any call for birthday cakes for *this* lot." Then he spotted a particular wizard among the throng. "Oh, except for Queequeg. Didn't see you over there. Happy birthday. I'd have gotten you a present, but I never much liked you anyway."

"ENOUGH!" Khosrau bellowed, and Jessie quaked in her sneakers. Mort could make light of these assholes all he wanted, but all it would take was one of them to burn her to cinders.

In fact, Mort appeared to be ready right that second to poke the proverbial bears that had them surrounded. "I'll say when it's enough. You probably wish you had a few more empty robes fluffing up your ranks. Bet you'd rather have them here than trying to shut down the saboteurs wreaking havoc on the whizzing little spaceships that keep Earth's weather tame."

The emperor turned to an adviser lurking near the throne. "You said he'd know better than to foul the planet's weather!"

Mort just smiled as he sauntered slowly toward the throne. Jessie edged along in his wake so as not to be too far from him when this inevitably went sour. "I do know better. But I just didn't care. The Order of Prometheus fell into line when I convinced them of my identity. I notice you didn't even try to recruit any to this doomed effort."

"YOU'RE ONE WIZARD!" Khosrau screamed. "The empire WILL NOT fall to one lone Convocation outcast!"

"Why not?" Aunt Tiffany interjected. "It did once before."

The emperor stared at the librarian's smirking face. "I'm counting on you!"

"Well, I'm counting me *out*. I returned to Earth because you needed me. I didn't sign up for this." With that, Tiffany headed for the nearest side door of the throne room.

One of the wizards on the dais, loitering in the wings, drew up a rebellious courage as well. He had all-black robes, ornately embroidered with mystical patterns that barely stood out in the monochrome palette. A face like someone who'd permanently lodged a lemon in his mouth barely twitched. "I, too, choose to adjourn myself from the proceedings. Mordecai, I bear you no ill will for deceiving me with your false demise."

"Someone stop them!" Khosrau ordered. When no one did so, he added a new invective. "Traitors!"

The pair faced no resistance, but that didn't stop Tiffany from offering a parting shot verbally. "Yeah, but who's going to walk out of here and blab about it?"

Towering, thick doors thundered shut behind them, and Jessie wondered whether she might have missed her chance to slink out on Aunt Tiffany's heels.

Khosrau's face was flushed with fury. "Blasted librarians! We still have enough arcane might to overpower him. I want no sorcery at work here but mine!"

Jessie felt a blanket of pressure thrown over her, so heavy that her feet could hardly move.

"It's not real," Mort informed her. "You can walk just fine. More importantly, it's me doing most of the holding at bay. This is an assemblage of doddering invalids and hotheaded blowhards. There's not a one of them that could run a mile without a pause for refreshment and rest, and nary a muscle strong enough to throw a punch that could daze you. Look inside. You still have your power."

Her power? Jessie was a kip-tie-mahl initiate. These were wizards from the Convocation, the backbone of the magical support for Emperor Khosrau Blackstone's rule. Any one of them ought to be able not only to render her powerless but run over her like a stuunji on the way to a free buffet.

Yet Jessie did as she was told. Using Master Bentho's pre-fight meditation training, she blocked out the world around her. Quiet amid angry, frightened voices. Weightless beneath a crushing load. Calm in the maelstrom.

Mort's words cut through her concentration. "Go ahead. Conquer Earth."

When she opened her eyes, Mort was under assault. Not by magic, which seemed impossible within his vicinity. Rather, dignified, stodgy men and women of the arcane arts rushed him, intent on bearing him down under a stampede of ineffectual noncombatants.

Jessie reacted.

Her body was spring-loaded. Her flesh was iron. Neither mongoose nor praying mantis could match her reflexes. She caught a wrist as its owner threw a lumbering punch Mort's way. Bone cracked. A wizard flew at the end of Jessie's kick.

Each punch ended a life.

Flying kicks propelled her to a new target with each fresh kill.

She dodged stabs from enchanted daggers and caught a runed sword between clapping palms before confiscating and ramming the blade through its owner's chest. Someone tried to sweep her feet from beneath her with a ceremonial staff, but she cartwheeled atop the haft and came away in possession of the weapon.

The bo staff wasn't her preferred close-combat weapon, but it had advantages over continuing to battle unarmed. Blows landed with the force of a cargo tram. Bodies crumpled. Jessie had to keep on the move simply to avoid being buried under the pile of corpses.

Why hadn't these fools simply fled?

When she had a fraction of a second to consider the question, the answer became obvious. Every door, every window to the throne room was aflame. She couldn't be certain when, but Mort had lost enough opposition to be able to work magic of his own.

Everything she knew about magic, everything Eric had told

her and Uncle Enzio and Aunt Tiffany and Aunt Esper and all the incidental acquaintances from chance meetings with spacers to Earth Navy colleagues said that two wizards countered one. Exceptions for the exceptional. Maybe a true force of supernature could thwart three or four peers. But there were still dozens of wizards alive and terrified and no doubt fervently wishing that someone might save them from Mordecai The Brown.

Not that it was *him* doing all the hard, bloody work here...

Jessie spared a glance to find her partner in crime swaggering up the steps of the dais.

Mort caught her eye and jerked a head to summon her over. "Care to witness history?"

"Little busy here," she called back. To emphasize her point, she planted a leaping kick to a wizard's chest that not only rammed him against a stone pillar but cracked the pillar with the force of the blow.

"Oh, you've done your part. Good work. Break time." With a snap of his fingers, Mort set the remaining opposition aflame. Wizards screamed and flailed, and Jessie scrambled to avoid getting burned by any of them.

On his throne, Emperor Khosrau was a cornered animal.

A lone wizard stepped forward to interpose himself, a last, sad, inadequate line of defense for the Emperor of Humankind.

"*Et tu*, Vincente?" Mort asked somberly.

"I am beholden to the empire, no one man."

Mort nodded. "Good last words." In a flash, the man was gone. No lingering flames tormented his final moments. Jessie suppressed a shudder at the ease with which that life had ended.

"I don't understand," Khosrau complained. "I have your friend. All you had to do was clean up Mars. You admitted wanting to do that anyway. All I did was incentivize you. You threw away Carl Ramsey's life... what... out of spite?"

Mort snickered. "Oh, I wager that a certain someone would like to continue receiving invites to holiday dinners, no matter how many of them she turns down. She's probably already wresting custody of Carl from my Brothers in Fire."

"And Azrael? He'd been nothing but loyal..."

"I know secrets about him that would unravel his life and legacy. And he knows I keep my word."

"But you broke an oath to me!"

Mort burst out laughing. Jessie couldn't recall Uncle Enzio ever being so merry. "I was standing in a warded circle at the time. Tell me the universe considers that anything more than bald-faced strategic deception. I gave you the galaxy. All you had to do was romp around your harem and make the occasional proclamation. You had to go biting the hand that fed you."

Khosrau shrank in his throne. "I'm your grandson. You wouldn't kill me?"

Jessie knew enough from Carl's stories that she knew Mort didn't place ties of blood over bonds of loyalty. "Maybe if you surrender formally and agree to step down, he'll—"

"Nah," Mort interrupted. Faster than Jessie could react, the wizard's fingers had clamped onto Khosrau's skull, penetrating knuckle-deep. There was a horrible hissing noise and a smell she hoped never to experience again. Dragging the body by the head, Mort made for the doors by which they'd entered. "Come on."

"What? Where are we going?"

"You're taking Carl and heading offworld. Hopefully with a chauffeur who owes me her life for leaving the doors unlocked for her exit. Me? I've got to convince someone to change their pants and fly me to Geneva."

As often as he tried to come up with original songs, Carl Ramsey's fingers slipped into familiar riffs and chords to timeless classics. Those old rock gods had just spoken to the galaxy and teased out the secrets of the soul. It wasn't Carl's fault that plagiarism was essentially a religious act.

He preferred to think of the pitcher of beer on his side table as half-empty, emptying being the goal of any container for alcohol. Bare feet rested on antique upholstery. He wasn't singing along to each track, but he tried to time his belches on the downbeat.

There was no knock before his door opened. Each guard and recurring visitor had some signature rapping that preceded them barging in. He considered that courtesy the key difference between house arrest and a posh dungeon.

"Ah. That explains it."

Tiffany Bell stood at his door, looking frazzled despite an outward bombast. "Let's get you out of here before the shitstorm really hits."

"I take it this didn't go the way you planned."

The librarian's scowl deepened. She didn't flinch when he met her gaze through those crystal lenses she wore to look more studious and less like an unemployed coffee addict with a teenager's fashion sense. "I was sent on a vacation to hide the fact you were being kept prisoner. And over in the other half of the palace, there's a mass murder taking place that I think I came within an offhand shrug of getting swept up in. So, no. Not my best day. Put some shoes on and grab your shit. We're leaving."

Carl slipped his feet into his boots as he sat up, not bothering to tie them. "This guitar was a gift."

"I don't give a shit. Grab a Rembrandt on your way out. Just move it, you tone-deaf old fuck."

That was a flippant, thoughtless, throw-away offer that Carl wasn't about to pass up. He'd been cooped up in this suite for weeks. From guards to kitchen staff, he'd talked the ear off anyone who'd listen. Innocuous conversations had to lay the groundwork for anything that might bear fruit over the course of a long escape scheme. That had included asking about every piece of artwork in the place.

Discarding the guitar he'd intended to steal, he clomped over to a painting on the wall. Twenty-second-century masterpiece by Ogdenburgh entitled *Blood of Charles*. Not Carl's can of beer, but the red-tone depiction of Boston Prime's major river and the surrounding city was worth a few hundred million, easy. Even at black market discounts. With an expert cracking of the frame, Carl rolled up the canvas in seconds.

"I really hate how you know how to do that," Tiffany commented as she leaned against the doorjamb.

"I wasn't always a respected member of the musical community."

The wizard snorted at that claim, then shrugged herself away from the wall and lead them out of the palace.

Carl didn't plan on heading back to Boston Prime—or Earth in general, for that matter—any time soon.

━━━

Charlotte marched through the corridors of the *Arete*, Jessie's boots stomping a drumbeat with Sparta's slippers providing syncopation. She'd have greatly appreciated access to her natural appearance right about now, but she was going to have to make do with maintaining her borrowed persona.

"If you're not comfortable with the plan, we can swap roles."

Slightly out of breath, Sparta shook her head. "No. I can do this. Mordecai trusted that I wouldn't need to hide beneath the hem of his robes. I won't prove him wrong."

There were two wizards out there, and if they encountered either of them, it wouldn't be their magical prowess saving anyone. Wits. The core of magical power since the dawn of time was knowing what your enemies didn't. Normally, that meant the delved secrets of the supernatural. Not always. Not today.

Charlotte couldn't say which of their foes she hoped to cross paths with. Neither, if she were honest with herself. A noble attempt bailed out by someone else risking their neck successfully ought to have suited her just fine.

"Ah. Captain." The voice chilled Charlotte to the bone. Azrin were typically unnerving up close. Daphne had inured her somewhat with her human mannerisms and gentle disposition. But Charlotte had grown up around members of the species who only spared her predation based on her mother's fearsome reputation.

Wizard Yarzzi Mekou slunk out of a side passage, hands out of his voluminous sleeves with palms upturned and claws out.

Charlotte drew up short. Sparta slid to a halt in her impractical footwear, pinwheeling her arms for balance to avoid either falling or venturing too close to their quarry.

If he *was* their quarry and not the other way around.

"Don't look so frightened," the azrin wizard cooed. "Two valuable and cooperative hostages would presently serve much better than a meal."

"You're no human-eater," Charlotte countered, taking a step back and barring the path to Sparta with an arm. Her other hand strayed toward a blaster sidearm that stood a Dane's chance in Hamlet of working.

"We don't need to consider the matter. Come with me. Ready a vessel to take us from here. You face no worse than house arrest on Earth."

Whether there was a grain of salt to that truth, the offer was reasonable on the face of it. An accomplished wizard against a mere oracle and a technologist? The odds favored the azrin so heavily that he could afford mercy.

"Take him out!" Charlotte ordered, allowing a tremor in her voice that the real Jessie couldn't have managed if she tried.

"What?" Sparta proclaimed.

"The thing!" Charlotte insisted. "Use the thing!"

"Oh, right. Sorry." The pair backed away, with Yarzzi matching them step for step, as Sparta fished in the bustline of her blouse. That particular detail had been added for the sake of the other wizard, the old man; Sparta hadn't the figure to be using her cleavage as a purse other than in an emergency. The fumbling was scripted, though the oracle's case of nerves appeared genuine. "Hah!"

Sparta presented the tiny, locked book like a crucifix before a vampire. It had about the same effect on the azrin, which was to say, none at all.

"What is that?" Wizard Yarzzi inquired, cocking his head as he approached. "A book of spells, or *prayers?*" He snickered at the joke. Certainly, if it were to be a battle of mystical prowess, Charlotte could feel the oppressive air that precluded her own use of magic.

"You-you-you-you're just going to find out the hard way," Sparta boasted as she fiddled with the lock. It released with a faint click.

The Convocation spy snarled and lunged. "Give that here!"

Sparta yipped and raised both hands, allowing the book to tumble from her fingers as she fled.

"Idiot!" Charlotte scolded as she dove for the prize.

Wizard Yarzzi was quicker, batting Charlotte aside with ease one-handed as he scooped up Sparta's fallen secret weapon with the other. "So, what have we here?"

He opened the cover.

Charlotte cringed in anticipation.

The azrin's eyes glazed over. His face contorted in pain and effort. Pages glowed, bathing Wizard Yarzzi's face in purple light. Runes projected on orange fur and unblinking eyes. The effort to break free was visible in every muscle and in the pitiful whimper.

With a sizzle, steam poured from the azrin's eyes, then smoke. Yarzzi collapsed to his knees, then fell forward, limp, onto his face. The book landed spine up, pages splayed against the floor.

Sparta crept close.

Charlotte grabbed her by the arm. "Leave it be!"

"It's fine," the oracle assured her, slipping free of a grip that didn't have Charlotte's full endorsement. She crouched and stretched out an arm, only glancing at her work from the corner of her eye. Pinching the book at the top and bottom of the spine, she gave a little shake as she lifted it, letting crumpled pages flatten out as the covers drooped closed. Not watching as she did so, Sparta snapped the clasp closed and locked. "Phew."

"And Mordecai found this piece of literature where, exactly?" Charlotte inquired.

"The book is a kids' diary he shoplifted from a gift shop in London Prime before we left Earth. I never saw the contents, but he wrote it himself."

Charlotte swallowed hard. Imagine the power. There were certainly wizards in the galaxy with whom she'd never wish to quarrel. But for one to dispatch an adversary in absentia like that...

"Glad he's on our side."

Sparta smirked and came damnably close to looking Charlotte in the eye. "He's on *my* side. Don't let that borrowed body fool yourself; there aren't a dozen people in the galaxy he truly gives a shit about."

Smoke still rose from the corpse of the azrin wizard. "We should find the other one. Can that book work twice?"

———

The directive from Commander Charlotte had been to spread out and search the whole of the *Arete*. While Grosstet respected the spirit of the order, there were days that his feet just didn't have a prolonged walk in them. Plus, the ship had better ways to find intruders than an exhaustive search.

Power.

The hoses throughout the ship fed every system from the weapons to the lifts, from the comms to the waste chutes. An advanced algorithm could compare typical power utilization against current usage and pick out the discrepancies.

But that was work for an engineer.

Grosstet was a people person.

He whacked a spot on the wall where he knew ventilation ducts ran behind. "I SEEK INFORMATION."

"Oh-hello-there-Commodore-Grosstet-How-can-I-be-of-assistance?"

Oh, how the little voices vexed him with their similarity and saddened him that he couldn't identify the speaker with any degree of certitude. Yet now wasn't the time for niceties. He had a ship in danger yet again. "I MUST FIND OUR

UNWELCOME GUESTS. DO YOU KNOW WHERE I MIGHT FIND ANY OR ALL OF THEM?"

A chorus of chittering too fast to pick out individual words echoed in the ducts.

"We've-got-a-five-seven-oh-at-Junction-40B-The-leader-of-the-envoys-representing-Earth's-interests-in-our-joint-venture."

"I THINK WE MAY SAFELY DROP THE PRETENSE OF COOPERATION WITH THEM."

"In-that-case-the-chief-spy-aboard-is-attempting-to-gain-access-to-human-sized-spaces-allowing-indirect-access-to-the-main-hangar-If-you-set-out-promptly-I-believe-you-can-intercept-him-before-he-gains-such-access."

"THANK YOU, FRIENDS."

Head held high, Grosstet sortied from his quarters in search of miscreants. For too long, the *Arete* and its crew had toyed with deception, and the house of smooth logs had finally wobbled. Now was the time for decisive action.

The human, Elgin Towers, would be forced to improvise and work around the unfamiliar systems of Grosstet's kind. Grosstet himself, however, could avail himself of the convenience of a lift ride that would put him quite close to his adversary. After all, lockouts didn't apply to *him* on his own ship.

That ride took mere moments.

Grosstet hadn't even brought along a weapon. Anything he might have used to any advantage might do more damage to the ship than to his tiny enemy.

Of course, he was no light-footed carnivore, either, to be prowling up on the unsuspecting and pounding without forewarning.

"AH, COMMANDER TOWERS," Grosstet called out, ensuring the human knew he was coming. "I HAVE SOUGHT YOU EVERYWHERE ELSE."

If his friendly demeanor bought him anything, it was time enough for the spy to pull a blaster. "Stay back. I need a comm channel and a ship. Provide both, and maybe our people can remain friends."

"DIPLOMACY AND DRAWN BLASTERS DO NOT MIX. DO YOU REALLY THINK THAT SMALL WEAPON WOULD HARM ME?" The haathee commodore didn't slow his approach.

Towers gave up on his efforts to pry open a section of wall with one of Jomek's hand tools and retreated down the corridor. "Maybe not. But this will." The human drew a slender device from his pocket, fiddled with it one-handed, and clamped a thumb down on one end. "This is an antimatter explosive. Enough mass to take out half this ship. If I take my thumb off the trigger, it'll detonate. That includes me going limp from unconsciousness or death."

Some of the human holovids had familiarized Grosstet with the concept. "AH. A DEAD-HUMAN SWITCH. THIS IS MY FIRST TIME ENCOUNTERING ONE IN A NONFICTIONAL SETTING."

"Then you know your only two choices are to get out of my way or force me to kill us all."

Grosstet chuckled.

"You think this is funny? You think I'd hesitate to use it?"

"I THINK YOU USE IT EACH DAY."

Towers froze.

Grosstet flapped his ears. "MY PEOPLE USE THE ANNIHILATION PARTICLES. I KNOW WELL THE SOUND THE CONTAINMENT FIELDS MAKE. WHAT YOU ARE HOLDING IS THE DEVICE YOU USE TO REMOVE THE HAIR THAT GROWS ON THE LOWER HALF OF YOUR FACE."

"Can you afford to risk that your guess is right?"

Grosstet laughed from his belly. "I AM NOT WRONG."

The human spy didn't hesitate. He turned and made a run for it.

There were two options here. He could content himself that he'd scared the spy into open flight, open a comm, and let the others know the path that the intruder had taken. Or, he could use his longer legs, overtake the little creature, and put an end to this all on his own.

Knees and hips and lower back lost the vote, and Grosstet burst into action.

Humans weren't especially quick creatures. Not like azrin. Not like ratatoret. While they claimed to be good long-distance runners, over a short sprint, plenty of species could overtake one.

Taking advantage of his size, Towers tried to use quick maneuvers to force Grosstet to lose ground getting his bulk to change direction. He dodged down every corridor, ducked under tables where lounges took up intersections, and knocked over flotsam the *Arete* crew had left lying around.

But the ship was simply too big. Too many wide, long spaces. Grosstet closed the distance, and just as Elgin Towers was about to disappear around yet another corner, the haathee dove.

An outstretched trunk wrapped around a thin, fragile waist.

He hadn't even meant to, but "careful" wasn't the watchword of Grosstet's pursuit. He heard the crack of ribs and vertebrae. A final gasp escaped involuntarily from his quarry.

When he let go, the body flopped limp into two distinct halves, and Grosstet looked around for somewhere to wash the blood off his trunk.

It was morning in Geneva Prime. Earth was in an uproar. Carl and Jessie had been whisked off the planet by a certain librarian who knew how to pick sides. A hasty convening of the full Earth Imperial Senate had taken some wrangling, but the work had been delegated, so it really hadn't been Mort's problem.

He'd gotten a good night's sleep, albeit a short one, and now his brethren from the Order of Prometheus stood guard around the senate building while Mort took the lectern to address the empire's legislative heart.

"Good morning, everyone. My name is Mordecai The Brown. Those of you who may once have known or *known of* me may note my youthful appearance with some skepticism. Death and I are old friends. This isn't my first return from apparent demise, and I promise you it won't be my last. Anyone who chooses not to believe my tale of reincarnation, let me assure you that I don't give a rat's ass.

"What's important is that I disposed of *this* fucker for you." Mort opened a palm and extended it toward the matching lectern beside his. Rather than a second representative or a debate opponent, as the setup might have indicated normally, the partner in this joint press conference was the lifeless body of Khosrau Blackstone, draped feet to one side with his head and arms dangling in full view of the senators and the cameras Mort was allowing to broadcast him galaxy-wide.

A furor arose from the senators. Mort quieted them with a spreading of his arms. "I am your avenging angel. I have delivered Earth and its colonies from the tyranny of imperial rule."

Hypocrite! A whiny voice accused from inside his head, where Mort was letting his grandson watch the proceedings. *This was you! It was all you!*

More shouts assailed Mort from the tiered gallery on all

sides. These were self-important humans, unaccustomed to patronizing.

"I'm not going to be taking over or anything so crass as that. There were laws and rights in place before Khosrau's Rebellion. They go back into effect immediately. With the current power vaccuum, we'll need some interim leadership. I hereby designate Chief Acquisitions Librarian Tiffany Bell as Transitional Regent. Rest assured, she doesn't want the job and will pass leadership of Earth to a successor as soon as one can be lawfully elected. The position of Convocation Grand Councilor will be granted to Azrael Copperfield. The Library of the Plundered Tomes having been instrumental in the preservation of pre-imperial tradition, these two will be essential in ensuring a return to more familiar times."

When more mutterings and shouted questions broke up the flow of Mort's pronouncements, he'd had his fill. "SILENCE!"

His voice rolled through the domed chamber like a clap of thunder.

Mort unfolded a sheet of parchment he'd scribbled on the way across the Atlantic last night. "I have here a list of names. When I read yours off, I want you to get up and leave the senate chamber. My associates from the Order of Prometheus will provide further instructions outside."

He then proceeded to call out the names of every miserable, annoying pain in his ass from his tenure in Khosrau Blackstone's body.

Nervous grumbles greeted the roll call. A few protested. Two had to be escorted out bodily.

When he'd finished the roster of anti-imperialist rabble-rousers, Mort smiled at the remaining senators. Nearly two-thirds still had their seats.

"There. Now that we're rid of those troublemakers, I'd like to thank the rest of you for your invaluable service in subjugating the empire and providing the illusion of normalcy and respectability to an abhorrent regime."

They did it for you! For US! What are you talking about?

Mort didn't need reminding that he'd fucked this all up. He'd only gone after Khosrau to punish him for murdering Nancy. Discovering Earth teetering on the brink of collapse and anarchy had tempted him. Mort had given in to every dark wizard's private little dream of conquering it all and ruling humanity with an iron fist. That was on him. Making amends required fixing the mistake. Nothing said *he* had to face consequences for it. That would have been nonsense.

Mort's reward for undoing the empire was getting away scot-free for starting it in the first place.

When the fires rose, he kept the temperature down. It would have been well within his power to melt the entire senate building into a puddle of molten ore and glass. But by next week, he hoped to have the senate reconvened with nothing but democracy activists and fresh appointees nominated with full understanding of what had become of their predecessors.

Oh, the screams were pitiable, but they were short-lived. Most of the holo-cams covering the proceedings even managed to keep their blinkies going throughout the inferno.

Yep.

Job well done.

That reminded Mort. Before he departed from Earth, he owed himself a good steak. Rare, though, not well done.

He'd earned it.

⬭

Charlotte sat with her ankles crossed, sipping a Darjeeling tea and watching the stars. Her quarters felt empty with Eric away.

Her nights flashed by in an instant, bolts of lightning with no thunder. Jessica's form still lingered, trapping her in an athletic frame and too much muscle, prone to excessive sweat. However, with the pretense of actually *being* Jessica Ramsey expired, she had no reason to dress in the captain's ill-cut uniforms. However, the captain owned nothing in the way of a comfortable daily-wear dress, and it wasn't worth the bother to have a new wardrobe printed for what promised to be a temporary problem.

At least, everyone *hoped* the situation would remain temporary.

Carl and Jessica Ramsey had rendezvoused with the *Scylla*. How long they lingered there was subject to whim, but gaining a second Jessie aboard the *Arete* would only add to the confusion. There was, as yet, no estimated arrival for Mordecai.

Maybe if the doppelganger effect *was* destined for an extended engagement, she'd arrange for a separate closet of clothes to distinguish between them. In the meantime, Charlotte enjoyed her tea while kitted out for a nice jog in matching *Arete* blue jumpsuit and sneakers.

The fact that no one had heard a peep from Eric worried her most.

He was supposed to have exited his Martian obligations and sent word from an obscure colony after muddling through his own means of egress. Charlotte had no doubt he could manage that much. Oh, perhaps he'd end up on a peanut farm in the League of Independent Planets or sleeping on a charity cot in some Seeker missionary outreach center in the border colonies. But he was a master—well, an aficionado, at least—of disguise.

And it wasn't as if their relationship could return to normal until she got her own body back. Not that they hadn't both experimented with being every living thing under the sun. But his own elder sister was a line she didn't care to venture across with him.

A soft rap at the door summoned Charlotte back from her own interior monologue.

"Enter."

Sparta swayed in, looking far more contented than before the downfall of Earth Empire. "You in a mood to be disturbed?"

"I'm poor company at the moment. I wouldn't mind inflicting my malaise on someone besides myself."

The oracle smiled. She'd come bearing a bottle of wine and noticed Charlotte's squinted attempt to read the label. "Just opinionated grape juice. More solace than celebration."

"I thought you were ironclad in your belief that Mordecai would be fine."

"I am. Eric, I worry about."

Charlotte swallowed a dry lump. "Kind of you. Few others seem concerned."

"Who counsels the counselor?"

"Eric," Charlotte declared without hesitation. "He's my permission to be... less than everything that's expected of me."

Sparta snickered. "Funny. My parents always wanted me to be a social climber. One of them must have owned a monkey's paw. I'm betrothed to a man who's conquered and thrown away an empire. He could command armies. He could order the stars to form new constellations. Yet none of that interests him."

"I wouldn't trade with you. It might earn me my mother's approval." Charlotte couldn't hold in her mirth and laughed at her own jest.

"Speaking of approval, are you a Convocation voter?"

Charlotte took custody of the wine bottle once Sparta opened it, taking the first drink. "Technically, I suppose. I've never exercised that prerogative."

"Well, if you change that, please resist any write-in campaigns drafting Mordecai for a senate seat."

"He doesn't seem like the sort who'd take such a position."

Sparta took back the bottle. "No. And he might hold a grudge against anyone who tries to make him."

"I'd consider it a fair trade for my original form back if I ignored the election entirely."

"Be nice of Mordecai to get back here and sort everything out for a happy homecoming for Eric. Or maybe he can break the enchantment himself."

There were many quirks of Eric's relationship with the universe. But convincing it to undo the will of Mordecai The Brown seemed unlikely to number among them.

"I do wonder what beneath the Martian skies Eric has gotten into that's keeping him from returning."

A dark, underground bunker beneath New Vancouver smelled of cheap coffee, men's aftershave, and expiring deodorant. Up and down the table, miniaturized medals gleamed on the breasts of uniforms bearing captains' and admirals' ranks in Mars Navy.

At the head of the table Supreme General Bob Randall held court.

"The bastards are trying to steal our thunder with an election of their own," the leader of Mars griped loudly enough for the Mars Marine Corps guards outside to overhear. "I don't know what their game is, but the possum emperor trick isn't fooling me."

A three-star admiral spoke up. "The intel *is* solid that Emperor Khosrau Blackstone was assassinated two days ago along with most of the senior members of the Convocation and his inner circle of advisers."

"According to who? To the enemy?" the supreme general countered. "None of our people has gotten a firsthand look. Place is locked down, burnt to a crisp, just the sort of scene you'd stage for an elaborate cover-up—the only kind of cover-up for something this momentous."

"If the reports are true, Earth has taken a serious blow to their magical protections."

"If they're true, they suggest the whole empire is adrift right now."

"Maybe the failed attack on the convention was their last gasp before total collapse."

The conversation volleyballed around the table from one side to the other, with nary an agreement, just more and more suggestions and wild speculation.

"What if this is the perfect time to pitch the idea of reunification?" Eric asked, taking what he felt was his turn.

All eyes up and down both sides of the table turned his way. Not that any of them *saw* Eric Ramsey. He was attending this meeting in the guise of Vice Admiral Stuart "Stooie" Quatermain. He was a legacy officer, promoted time and again because everyone liked to curry favor with a family that had been serving humankind's Black Ocean navies since they were launched. In the short time he'd been impersonating the guy, extenuating circumstances of the present crisis had given him not only the excuse of "not feeling like himself" but also the impression that not many people took Stooie Quatermain too seriously.

But he got invited to meetings.

Eric couldn't account for exactly how he'd ended up in this one, but his panicked flight from New Vancouver Civic Arena had required the hasty switching of identities with someone, and the vice admiral had been in his path when Eric wasn't looking where he was going.

Supreme General Randall himself broke the ensuing silence in the wake of Eric's suggestion. "Stooie, you'd better be talking about Earth's surrender and none of that cockamamie olive branch bullshit they're pitching on the feeds."

Eric gulped. He wasn't here to rock boats.

"Oh, yeah. Naturally. I mean, Earth is in chaos. I think if someone made them the offer, maybe surrender is on the table."

The real Stooie Quatermain was a resident of a custom-made little world in the Village of Eternity. In it, he was attending this same meeting in fits and starts as Eric ground time to nearly outside-world speeds. Every reaction was vetted, tested, and certified by the man himself before Eric spoke it aloud.

Up until his offhanded suggestion about peace with Earth, at any rate.

"Well... maybe we'll run it past a few analysts. See what the computers say. I think the number one thing we need right *now*, though, is a plan to hit Earth fast and hard, right where it hurts." Heads nodded. A few admirals and a marine general agreed out loud. Nobody wanted to oppose the supreme general.

Eric just wanted to find a way home.

But he couldn't leave Mars such a mess. This was his fault, and he needed to do something about it.

He'd missed his chance to free Mars in one fell swoop, and he hadn't pre-arranged a time loop to try again.

If only there were some other way.

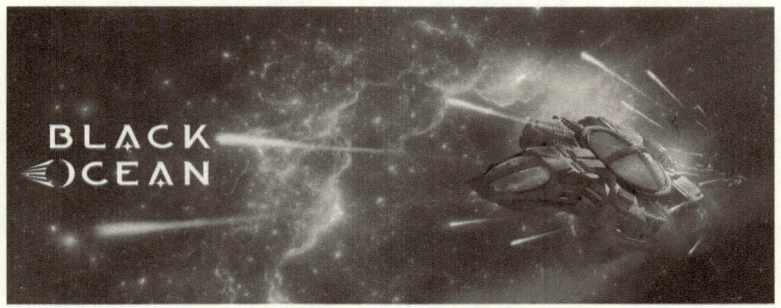

Black Ocean

Black Ocean is a vivid 26th century story universe where science and magic coexist—sort of.

Black Ocean: Galaxy Outlaws (16 missions)

Black Ocean: Galaxy Outlaws is a fast-paced fantasy space opera series about the small crew of the *Mobius* trying to squeeze out a living. If you love fantasy and sci-fi, and still lament over the cancellation of *Firefly*, *Black Ocean: Galaxy Outlaws* is the series for you.

Read about the *Black Ocean: Galaxy Outlaws* series and discover where to buy at: galaxyoutlawsmissions.com

Black Ocean: Astral Prime (12 missions)

Co-written with author M.A. Larkin, *Black Ocean: Astral Prime* hearkens back to location-based space sci-fi classics like *Babylon 5* and *Star Trek: Deep Space Nine*. *Astral Prime* builds on the rich *Black Ocean* universe, introducing a colorful cast of characters for new and returning readers alike. Come along for the ride as a minor outpost in the middle of nowhere becomes a key point of interstellar conflict.

Read about the *Black Ocean: Astral Prime* series and discover where to buy at: astralprimemissions.com

Black Ocean: Mercy for Hire (16 missions)

Black Ocean: Mercy for Hire follows the exploits of a pair of do-gooder bounty hunters who care more about saving the day than securing a payday. The series builds on the rich *Black Ocean* universe, centering on a couple of fan-favorites and introducing a colorful cast for new and returning readers alike. Fans of vigilante justice and heroes who exemplify the word will love this series.

Read about *Black Ocean: Mercy for Hire* and discover where to buy at: mercyforhiremissions.com

Black Ocean: Mirth & Mayhem (16 missions)

Black Ocean: Mirth & Mayhem delves into the origins of two vagabonds making their living among the stars. Mort is a wizard coming to grips with a life on the run and estrangement from the comforts and respect he had on Earth. Brad is an impressionable youth, too clever for his—or anyone's—good. And Chuck Ramsey is the mold that Brad's trying to break out of, which is harder than he could ever have dreamed.

Read about *Black Ocean: Mirth & Mayhem* and discover where to buy at: mirthandmayhemmissions.com

Black Ocean: Passage of Time (in-progress)

The year was 2586. A few minutes later, it was 2591. Caught up in a time travel snafu, Eric and Jessie Ramsey become fugitives from the people who want answers as to how they did it—and where their loyalties lie in the galactic war that broke out in their absence.

Read about *Black Ocean: Passage of Time* and discover where to buy at: passageoftimemissions.com

Black Ocean Fan Group

Join the *Black Ocean* Facebook fan group to discuss *Black Ocean* with other outlaws. Chat about ebooks, audio, or paper versions; main series or spin-offs; or share photos of the pet you named after Kubu.

Request to join at: <u>blackoceanfans.com</u>

Black Ocean Merch

Wish you could live in the Black Ocean world?

I can't promise you'll win an argument with the universe, but you CAN wear your own wizard hoodie (adorned with Convocation medallion), disguise your boring 21st-century soda or beer with the Earth's Preferred can cooler, or fly the Poet Fleet Jolly Roger.

Browse merch at: <u>blackoceangear.com</u>

Twinborn Chronicles

The *Twinborn Chronicles* is an epic fantasy saga based on the possibility that our dreams offer us a glimpse into the life of another – another who can get the same glimpse into our world.

Read about the *Twinborn Chronicles* and discover where to buy at: twinbornchronicles.com

Twinborn Chronicles: Awakening

Experience the journey of mundane scribe Kyrus Hinterdale who discovers what it means to be Twinborn—and the dangers of getting caught using magic in a world that thinks it exists only in children's stories.

Twinborn Chronicles: War of 3 Worlds

Then continue on into the world of Korr, where the Mad Tinker and his daughter try to save the humans from the oppressive race of Kuduks. When their war spills over into both Tellurak and Veydrus, what alliances will they need to forge to make sure the right side wins?

Project Transhuman: Eve14

Project Transhuman brings genetic engineering into a post-apocalyptic Earth, 1000 years aliens obliterated all life.

These days, even the humans are built by robots.

Charlie7 is the oldest robot alive. He's seen everything from the fall of mankind at the hands of alien invaders to the rebuilding of a living world from the algae up. But what he hasn't seen in over a thousand years is a healthy, intelligent human. When Eve stumbles into his life, the old robot finally has something worth coming out of retirement for: someone to protect.

Read about all of the *Project Transhuman* books and discover where to buy at: projecttranshuman.com

OTHER BOOKS BY J. S. MORIN

Sins of Angels

Co-written with author M.A. Larkin, *Sins of Angels* is an epic space opera series set 3000 years after the fall of Earth. With the scope of *Dune* and the adventurous spirit of *Indiana Jones*, it delivers a conflict that spans galaxies and rests on the spirit of brave researcher Professor Rachel Jordan. Follow the complete saga, and watch as the fate of our species hangs in the balance.

Read about *Sins of Angels* and discover where to buy at: sinsofangelsbooks.com

Shadowblood Heir

Shadowblood Heir explores what would happen if the writer of your favorite epic fantasy TV show died before the show ended—and the show was responsible. If you wonder what it would be like if an epic fantasy world invaded our world, this urban fantasy story might give you that glimpse.

Read about *Shadowblood Heir* and discover where to buy at: shadowbloodheir.com

EMAIL INSIDERS

You made it to the end! Maybe you're just persistent, but hopefully that means you enjoyed the book. But this is just the end of one story. If you'd like reading my books, there are always more on the way!

Perks of being an Email Insider include:

- Inside track on beta reading and advance review copies (ARCs)
- Access to Inside Exclusive bonus extras and giveaways
- Best of my blog about fantasy and science fiction topics

Sign up for the my Email Insiders list at: jsmorin.com/updates

ABOUT THE AUTHOR

I am a creator of worlds and a destroyer of words. As a fantasy writer, my works range from traditional epics to futuristic fantasy with starships. I have worked as an unpaid Little League pitcher, a cashier, a student library aide, a factory grunt, a cubicle drone, and an engineer—there is some overlap in the last two.

Through it all, though, I was always a storyteller. Eventually I started writing books based on the stray stories in my head, and people kept telling me to write more of them. Now, that's all I do for a living.

I enjoy strategy, worldbuilding, and the fantasy author's privilege to make up words. I am a gamer, a joker, and a thinker of sideways thoughts. But I don't dance, can't sing, and my best artistic efforts fall short of your average notebook doodle. When you read my books, you are seeing me at my best.

Connect with me online
jsmorin.com

facebook.com/authorjsmorin

bookbub.com/authors/j-s-morin

youtube.com/@authorjsmorin

www.ingramcontent.com/pod-product-compliance
Lightning Source LLC
Chambersburg PA
CBHW032009240626
47153CB00003B/1184